Two Souls Hollow

PAULA GRAVES

MILLS & BOON

First published in Great Britain 2015
by Mills & Boon, an imprint of Harlequin (UK) Limited,
Large Print edition 2015
Eton House, 18-24 Paradise Road,
Richmond, Surrey, TW9 1SR

© 2015 Paula Graves

ISBN: 978-0-263-26019-9

Harlequin (UK) Limited's policy is to use papers that are natural, renewable and recyclable products and made from wood grown in sustainable forests. The logging and manufacturing processes conform to the legal environmental regulations of the country of origin.

Printed and bound in Great Britain
by CPI Antony Rowe, Chippenham, Wiltshire

As she started to speak, he heard the sound of shattering glass coming from somewhere in the house.

It was apparently loud enough to carry through the phone, because a moment later, Ginny asked, "What was that?"

"I'm not sure," he answered, keeping his voice low. He stepped out of her room into the hall. From there, he could see into the kitchen. Nothing seemed out of place.

Then he heard the sound of more glass breaking, coming from the front of the house. Glass clattered onto a hard surface, then a second later came the unmistakable crunch of glass being broken underfoot.

"Anson?" Ginny's voice rose in his ear.

He ducked back into her bedroom and eased the door closed, his heart pounding. "Someone's breaking into your house."

PAULA GRAVES,

an Alabama native, wrote her first book at the age of six. A voracious reader, Paula loves books that pair tantalising mystery with compelling romance. When she's not reading or writing, she works as a creative director for a Birmingham advertising agency and spends time with her family and friends. Paula invites readers to visit her website, paulagraves.com

For my buddy Paul,
whose sweetness is eclipsed
only by his geektastic awesomeness.

Chapter One

Kittens. Bunnies. Lemon icebox pie with whipped cream. The real stuff, not that gunk that came out of a can.

That was Ginny Coltrane. Soft, sweet and delicious.

So what the hell was she doing walking into the seediest bar in Ridge County?

Anson Daughtry's cell phone buzzed. He glanced at the display and grimaced as he answered. "Hey, boss. Can I still call you that? This whole administrative-leave thing is a little confusing."

"I'm still writing your paychecks," Alexander Quinn answered in that toneless voice he used when he didn't want to let anyone know what he was really feeling. Of course, that usually meant he was ticked off and didn't want to give anyone the pleasure of knowing it. Anson took a certain amount of satisfaction in knowing he could get to the unflappable ex-CIA agent that way. Felt like a victory, and he'd had damned few of those in recent days.

"Boss it is, then."

"I wanted to let you know I've taken Darcy off administrative leave."

Keeping his eyes on the entrance of the Whiskey Road Tavern, Anson tried to keep any hint of emotion out of his own voice. "Already heard."

"You're angry."

So much for keeping emotion out of his voice. "Don't know why you'd say that. I mean, it's not like I'm now your prime suspect for corporate espionage or anything."

"I have to go through the process."

"And Darcy gets a free pass why?" Anson stopped trying to hide his bitterness. Quinn would see through him anyway. "Because he saved an FBI agent in trouble and fed her corrupt supervisor to the band of domestic terrorists the man was trying to use for his own purposes? Stupid me, not stumbling into a chance to play hero and win your approval."

"Get over yourself, Daughtry. Unless you'd like me to cut you loose and let you see how easy it is to find another job with a cloud of suspicion hanging over your head?"

He hated when Quinn got haughty. And the temptation to turn in his resignation, regardless of how hard it made his life, was almost more than he could resist. He'd never been much of a joiner anyway.

But an IT job at a commercial company would bore him senseless. And he'd worked for law-enforcement agencies before and quickly discovered he was ill-suited for the law-and-order mind-set.

He was a cyber cowboy, he thought with a wry grin. And the high-stakes security firm known as The Gates was Anson's version of the Wild,

Wild West. Hell if he'd let anyone drive him out on false charges.

"Fine. Darcy is cleared. I'm not. Is that the only reason you called?"

"I hoped, in vain, to reach you before you'd heard." Quinn's voice lowered. "And to make sure you understand that this suspension is not an indication of my own opinion about your guilt or innocence."

"You believe in me so much you're extending my paid vacation? I'm touched."

"I realize it's hard to believe this, but I am not your enemy."

The front door of the Whiskey Road Tavern opened and Ginny Coltrane exited, her arm around the waist of a tall dark-haired man. He leaned heavily on her, clearly not in complete control of his motor skills, as she guided him toward her little blue Ford Focus.

Anson leaned toward the windshield of his own car, trying to get a better look in the blue glow of the streetlamp. What was a sweet little gumdrop like Ginny Coltrane doing hauling a strapping hunk of a drunk out of a notorious mountain honky-tonk?

Boyfriend?

"Daughtry?" Quinn's voice rose in his ear, and he realized his boss had been repeating his name.

"Yeah, gotta go, Quinn." He hung up and watched Ginny try to squeeze the slobbering drunk into the passenger seat of the Ford. He wasn't cooperating much, reaching up to grab her face and grinning like an inebriated ass.

Anson had his hand on the door handle before he stopped himself. He couldn't exactly rush to her rescue, could he? He certainly didn't want her knowing he was following her around like some kind of stalker.

Which he wasn't. Not at all. Lemon icebox pie with whipped cream was entirely too rich and sweet for a guy like him. He had other reasons for tailing her.

He watched as Ginny finished folding her drunk companion into the passenger seat and closed the door behind her. Pushing her mussed hair out of her eyes, she started to go around the car to the driver's side when four dark shadows emerged from the woods that edged that end of the tavern's parking lot. The shadows materialized into four large men clad in dark clothing. Before Ginny could react, they surrounded her in a menacing semicircle, trapping her against the side of the car.

Anson muttered a low curse and opened the car door, wishing he'd paid better attention at those company threat-containment training seminars. Quinn was a stickler about training everybody in his agency in self-defense and dealing with crisis situations, even support staff and people like Anson, who never went out into the field.

One thing he knew without a doubt—no way in hell could he take on four burly thugs and win. Just one, and he might have a fighting chance. He might not be some muscle-bound special agent like some of the guys at The Gates, but he was fit, strong and agile. And while he preferred to defuse a tense situation rather than resorting to violence if he could, he'd survived his share of fights over the years.

But not four against one.

Don't look like a threat, especially if you're not. Quinn's words came back to him as he looked across the narrow parking lot at the four men closing in on Ginny Coltrane.

Yeah, got that one handled, he thought, catching a glimpse of himself in the reflection in his car window. Tall, lean, with brown hair falling over his forehead and his Weezer T-shirt about three sizes too large, making him look thinner than he was.

"Hey, Ginny!" he called out, slouching his way across the parking lot toward her and the men.

Ginny's head swiveled, her big blue eyes meeting his, first with hope, then with dismay. Her brow furrowed, the last bit of hope fading from her expression.

Gee, thanks, sweetness. But he kept moving, ignoring the men. "I'm sorry I'm late—I guess you almost gave up on me," he continued, pointedly ignoring the four men.

They didn't ignore him. "Get lost," one of them growled.

He stopped short, looking straight at the man who'd spoken. His direct gaze seemed to catch the man by surprise. "Oh, am I interrupting? Oh, man, I'm sorry. Go ahead. I'll wait. Since I was late anyway."

He pulled his phone from his pocket and pulled up his Twitter account.

If I die today, 4 burly men @ the Whiskey Road Tavern did it. Check security vid. If 1 exists.

"No, you're not interrupting," Ginny said. "These fellows were just leaving."

He glanced at her, surprised by her forceful tone. The Ginny he knew from the office was quiet and unassuming. Pretty as a sunny day but some people missed that about her because they never even really saw her.

"I'm glad you made it," she added with a bright

smile at him, moving slowly around the nearest of the four men and walking toward Anson at a bravely unhurried pace.

He kept his eyes on her, trying not to worry about what the men were doing. As long as she made it to his side and he had a chance to get her out of danger, that was all that mattered. Identifying those men could come later, if at all.

He held out his palm to her. She reached out her small hand and grabbed his. Her fingers were cool. Soft to the touch. But her grip was strong. He felt something warm and unexpected rip its way through his chest. Something he really didn't want to examine, especially not with four big men bearing down on them.

He bent and kissed her cheek, feeling her tremble beneath that light caress. She smelled soap-and-water clean, the delicate scent filling his lungs and threatening to eclipse everything but the sweet heat of her body curving close to his. "Who's the guy in the car?" he murmured in her ear.

"My brother," she answered, brushing her lips against his jawline.

His heart skipped a couple of beats. He wanted to chalk it up to the tense situation, but he wasn't an idiot.

Ginny Coltrane wasn't lemon icebox pie, after all. Maybe more of a dark-chocolate truffle.

Wait. Her brother?

He looked up to see the four men moving toward them, faster than he'd hoped. "Go back into the bar," he murmured to Ginny. "The bartender's name is Jase. Tell him I need help out here."

She looked up at him, her brow furrowed. "What's your name again?"

Well. That was nice, wasn't it?

"Anson Daughtry."

She made an apologetic face. "Right. I knew that."

"Go now." He walked with her part of the way, acutely aware of the sound of footsteps hurrying across the gravel parking lot toward them. "Go!"

Ginny started running toward the front door of

the bar. One of the big men peeled away toward her, giving Anson no choice.

He ran toward the man in high gear, his long legs eating up the distance between them. His move seemed to catch the other men by surprise; he felt the whoosh of air as they grabbed for him and missed. He hit his target hard, pain ratcheting through his chest as his sternum collided with the man's thick-muscled arm. He wrapped his arms around the man's body, not stopping the bearded man's forward movement but slowing it down just enough for Ginny to disappear safely through the bar entrance.

Anson let go and dropped to the gravel in front of the man, tripping him up. He hit Anson on the way to the ground, his knee slamming into Anson's side, driving the air from his lungs. Rolling into a ball, Anson struggled to breathe, his chest on fire. It seemed to take several long minutes before he finally sucked in a lungful of cool night air.

Just in time to take a steel-toed boot right to the rib cage.

Son of a *bitch*, that hurt!

THERE WAS NOBODY tending bar. How could there be nobody tending bar in a tavern?

Ginny skidded to a stop in front of the bar, suddenly aware of the roomful of eyes watching her dash across the sawdust-strewn floor. They didn't scare her, those hard, suspicious men. She'd grown up among them, knew how they thought.

But those men outside—they were different. Cold-eyed. Purposeful.

And she'd left that poor computer guy from The Gates out there to deal with them.

"Jase!" she yelled. "Jase!"

A man approximately the size of Chimney Rock rose from a crouch behind the bar and gave her a puzzled look. "You're back."

"Anson Daughtry is outside. There are four big guys beating up on him. He needs your help."

Jase was around the bar in seconds, slapping men on the back as he moved toward the door. Each of the men he touched rose and got in line behind him, heading out into the parking lot.

Ginny fell in step with them, bringing up the rear. By the time she was out the door, there was no sign of the four men who'd surrounded her car.

But Anson Daughtry lay curled up on the gravel parking lot, bleeding from his nose.

Without anyone to fight, the men from the bar stopped short of the man writhing in pain on the ground as if uncertain how to proceed. Ginny pushed past them with a growl of frustration and crouched beside Anson, pushing his hair away from his face.

He'd taken a few blows to the face, his cheek bruised and swollen, blood still dripping from both nostrils. One of his eyes looked puffy. And his breathing was labored.

"Call 9-1-1," she ordered the nearest man.

"No," Anson said, his voice pained. "I'm not

that badly hurt. Just give me a second to catch my breath."

She shot a hard look at the man she'd just addressed. "Don't be an idiot. He's injured and probably concussed. Go call 9-1-1 like I asked."

The man gave a gruff reply. "I don't have a phone."

"I do," another offered, though he didn't pull it out to start making the call.

She shot him a hard glare. "Call 9-1-1," she said with the firmness of a mother scolding a child. The man quickly pulled out his phone and started dialing.

"You sounded just like a mom." Anson's words came out thick-tongued. "I almost crawled back to the car for my own phone."

Her soft, involuntary laugh caught her by surprise, because mirth was the last thing she felt at the moment. "Lie still and try not to talk. I need to go check on Danny."

"Your brother?"

He remembered that much, she thought, relieved. "Yes. He's…indisposed."

"Yeah, my dad used to spend a lot of his time indisposed, too." Anson pushed himself up to a sitting position, groaning. "Those bast—jerks kicked me in the ribs."

"You can say *bastards* in front of me," she said quietly, cupping his chin with her fingers to get a better look at his battered face. "Since I am one—"

His eyes flicked open wider. Well, one of them did. The other was quickly beginning to swell shut.

She couldn't stop a slight smile at his surprise. She was used to being underestimated. "How's your breathing?"

"Better now that I don't have boots hammering my rib cage into my lungs." He wiped his bloody nose with his shirtsleeve, looking down at the red stain as if surprised to see it. "You should probably check on your brother. I think one of the guys went over to talk to him."

Right. Her brother.

She pushed to her feet, surprised to feel reluctance as she left his side and headed to her car, keeping an eye on the encroaching woods as she circled to the passenger side. There were plenty of gloomy shadows, but no signs of anyone moving around among the trees.

She squelched a shiver. Who the hell were those guys? And what had they wanted? Was it something to do with Danny?

The car was listing to one side, she noticed as she reached for the door handle. With dismay, she saw that the tires had been slashed on the passenger side. She'd have to call road service for a tow.

"Gigi!" Danny greeted her with a sloppy grin when she opened the passenger door to check on him. He'd attempted to buckle himself in, but he'd fastened the belt just below his breastbone. He had his arms folded over his stomach as if he was cold. Which he probably was. May had finally arrived in the Smoky Mountains, but the chill of spring still clung to the night air. "Are we home yet?"

The urge to cry nearly overwhelmed her. "Not yet."

"I'll just sleep a little longer." His head lolled back against the seat.

She closed the car door and hurried back to Anson Daughtry. He was on his feet, she saw with dismay. Swaying a little, as if buffeted by the brisk night breeze blowing through the trees around them. But upright for now, at least.

She directed a stern look at Jase, who seemed to be the one person the other men looked at with respect. "We should get him inside so he can sit down while we wait for the paramedics."

"He made us call back and cancel the 9-1-1 emergency," Jase said quickly. "All his idea."

"Traitor," Anson muttered, dabbing his bloody nose with a grimy-looking handkerchief someone had supplied while she was checking on Danny.

"You afraid of doctors?" she asked.

"No."

"Needles?"

He shook his head.

"Sterile environments?"

He made a skeptical face. "Do you know how many germs there are floating around the average hospital?"

Great. A quick-witted smart-ass. Just her luck.

"I'm okay," he said, his expression suddenly serious. "Bruises and contusions, but nothing seems to be broken." He gave a brief nod toward Jase. "Thanks, man, I owe you."

Jase shrugged. "I'll let you know when the wife's laptop goes on the blink." He nodded to the other men and they all headed back into the bar.

"He seems an odd friend for you," Ginny said.

Anson managed a lopsided grin. "I'm an odd-friend connoisseur. Kind of a hobby."

"Thank you for tonight. I don't know who those guys were or what they were up to, but it clearly wasn't anything good."

He glanced toward her car. "Did you ask your brother if he knew them?"

She didn't miss the implication. "He barely recognizes me when—"

"When he's indisposed," he supplied.

She nodded. "I need to call for a tow. They seem to have slashed my tires as they left."

"Strange."

"Are you sure you're okay? Maybe we should call—"

"I'm fine." He offered another pained smile.

"You should at least stop by the after-hours clinic in town. Let them look you over, make sure you don't have any internal injuries."

He nodded but didn't speak. She could tell he had no intention of taking her advice. She was used to that, as well.

"Really lucky for me you were here," she added.

Something shifted in his expression. She couldn't quite read the quicksilver emotion, but it piqued her curiosity. She immediately shoved aside the momentary flicker of interest—she might work at a private investigation and security agency, but the last thing she needed in her life was more intrigue.

Besides, Anson Daughtry was in some sort of trouble at The Gates, wasn't he? He'd been put on administrative leave for some reason.

"Consider the clinic," she added as a parting shot, then headed back to the car to check on Danny and call for a tow truck.

Danny's head rolled toward her as she slid behind the steering wheel and gripped it with her suddenly shaking hands. She'd been as solid as steel through most of the past few minutes, but apparently her adrenaline spike had passed, leaving her feeling shivery and enervated.

"Gigi," he murmured, sounding distressed.

As she turned to look at him, the dome light that had come on when she opened the driver's door turned off, and she got only a quick glimpse of something dark staining the front of his shirt. For a moment, she felt an old, familiar hardness stiffen her spine. He'd thrown up his night's liquid intake all over himself and her car.

Except she wasn't smelling vomit and liquor.

The odor was sharper. More metallic.

She opened the door, engaging the dome light and, for a long moment, simply stared without comprehension at the wet red stain spreading across the front of Danny's shirt. It had been hidden under his folded arms before, she realized.

Danny gazed at her, his expression twisted with fear and pain. "Gigi?"

She dug for her phone and dialed 9-1-1.

Chapter Two

Anson entered the emergency room waiting area and acquired his target in seconds, despite the crowd of people filling the chairs and sofas scattered around the room. She sat in the corner, an island of stillness in a kinetic sea of anxiety, her blond hair now finger-combed into some sort of order and her hands folded serenely in her lap.

But as her soft blue eyes flicked up to meet his, he saw the terror her placid facade was hiding.

"Did you get checked out?" Her voice was low and tight.

"Yeah. Nothing broken. Didn't even need stitches in my cheek." The cut under his black eye was hurting like hell, but he refrained from whining about it, under the circumstances. "Any word on your brother?"

She shook her head. "I'm hoping no news is good news."

"It might be." He waved at the seat beside her. "Okay if I sit?"

"Of course." She edged over as if to give him extra room. He sat beside her, taking care not to touch her. He had the strangest feeling that if he touched her, she would shatter.

"Thank you for the ride," she added. "I really didn't want to catch a ride with the cops."

He touched his swollen nose with his fingertips, wincing at the inevitable pain. "You got warrants out on you or something?"

"No." She answered as if it were a serious question.

Her response intrigued him, but he tabled his curiosity for later. "They'll probably have more questions. They're lurking near the exam rooms right now, I guess waiting for a chance to interview your brother."

"It won't do them much good. He's not sober enough to make any sense anyway." A touch of bitterness darkened her voice. She seemed to hear it herself, her expression icing over and her posture stiffening. "You probably want to get home. I can call a cab or something."

"I'm in no hurry to get home." He started to settle his long limbs more comfortably in the chair beside her, then stopped short. "Unless you want me to leave?"

She gave him a long, considering look that made him feel as if he were undergoing some sort of silent assessment. Finally, she shook her head. "I don't mind the company."

Ringing endorsement, that. He stretched his legs out and attempted to get a little more comfortable.

After a few minutes she broke the silence. "Did the police talk to you about those men?"

"They did."

"Do you think you could identify them from a lineup?"

She sounded so hopeful, he hated to answer truthfully. "I didn't get a very good look at any of them. I was focused on getting you clear of them, and after that, I was pretty much on the ground with my arms around my head having the hell kicked out of me."

She winced. "I'm so sorry about that."

"Not your fault."

"I can't get over how lucky I was that you were there. It was really brave of you to come to my rescue that way."

The tentative smile she flashed at him felt like sunshine and rainbows and fireworks exploding, and he felt like a complete idiot for the direction of his thoughts. "Isn't that sort of the company motto? All for one and one for all?"

"I think that's *The Three Musketeers*."

"Great book."

"But a sadly flawed movie."

"Which one?" He slanted a look at her.

"Any of them."

That did it. He was in geek love.

"I guess I need to call Mr. Quinn and let him know I'll be late coming in tomorrow morning." She looked at her watch, frowning. "It's after ten."

"Quinn never sleeps. I think he's a vampire."

Her startled laughter sounded like music.

Oh, God, he had to stop thinking like that.

"I can call him for you," he offered. "We're tight."

"Oh, is that why he put you on administrative leave?" she asked tartly.

Uh-oh, she had a sassy side. He was in trouble now. "Yeah, he loves me. All these days off with pay. I'm a lucky guy."

"There's an internal investigation, right?" She gave him another side-eyed look. "Something about information leaks?"

There was an odd tone to her voice that once again tugged at his curiosity. But before he could answer, the door to the waiting room opened, and every eye in the place focused on the man in the green scrubs who walked through the opening.

"Ms. Coltrane?"

As the others in the waiting room slumped back into miserable anticipation, Ginny stood up, her spine straight and her head high as the doctor approached her. Only the clenching and unclenching of her hands gave any indication of her stress.

"I'm Ginny Coltrane." Her voice was clear. Strong. Anson marveled at her composure, because his own gut was twisting into knots of anxiety as he waited for the doctor to speak.

"I'm Dr. Emerson. I'm the attending physician for your brother, Daniel. Your brother suffered a single penetrating stab wound to the upper-right abdomen. The good news is that the blade missed any major blood vessels and the lungs. But he does have a liver laceration that has us worried, especially given his blood-alcohol level. Does he have a history of liver disease?"

Ginny glanced at Anson before she spoke. "He— Not that I know of. But he is a heavy drinker."

The doctor nodded. "He's young and relatively

healthy, and the liver injury should heal on its own without further intervention, but we'll want to keep him here a few days for observation."

Anson could tell from the doctor's tone that a big part of the "observation" would be to make sure Danny Coltrane didn't try to filter any more liquor through his injured liver before it had a little time to heal.

Ginny knew it, too. He could see the misery in her eyes as she nodded. "I think that's a good idea."

"We can't force him to stay if he decides to disregard our medical advice," Dr. Emerson warned. "You may need to speak to him about the importance of letting us do our jobs."

"I know. I'll speak to him." She smiled at the doctor, but there was no relief in her expression, only a miserable fragility that elicited a deep ache in the center of Anson's chest.

"Right now, he's sleeping, but if you want to go see him before we transfer him to a room—"

"Yes," she said. "Thank you."

Dr. Emerson looked at Anson. "If you wish, your friend can go with you. There are a couple of chairs in the exam room."

Anson started to demur, but Ginny looked at him with those misery-filled baby blues and he was ready to follow her into a raging fire if she needed him to.

What the hell was wrong with him?

"Thank you," she told Dr. Emerson, still looking at Anson.

He rose and stood beside her, tall and gangly to her small and composed, and he felt the sudden, uncomfortable sense that he had been sucked into something entirely outside his realm of experience.

And since he considered himself something of a Renaissance man, the sensation was discomfiting indeed.

After the doctor left, the frozen mask of composure on Ginny's face slipped, just a bit, revealing her raw anxiety. "You don't have to come with me. I'm sorry. I shouldn't have—"

"I'll go with you," he said.

The look of grateful relief on her face elicited another throbbing ache in the center of his breastbone. "He can be hard to deal with at the best of times."

"He's your younger brother?"

She shook her head, her voice bleak. "Older. But he's my responsibility anyway."

"Why?"

She shot him a frowning look, as if confused by the question. "Because he's family."

Of course, Anson thought. *Family.*

He should have known.

Except he'd never really had one.

DANNY LOOKED SO PALE. So small, somehow, even though he was a big guy, a little on the lean side due to drinking too much and eating too little, but at twenty-eight, the liquor hadn't really started taking a toll on his health yet.

But it was coming. Ginny had seen it in the

doctor's eyes when he told her about Danny's condition.

He was sleeping peacefully enough, so she didn't try to wake him. They could talk when he was in his own room and sober enough to hear what she had to say.

She stepped away from the gurney where Danny lay and turned to look at Anson Daughtry. He looked entirely too large for the small metal chair onto which he'd folded his lanky frame, all arms and legs and broad shoulders. He looked up at her with such a soft expression that she felt the absurd urge to throw her arms around his waist and cry against his chest.

He'd wrap those long arms around her and say nice, comforting things to her, and maybe, just maybe, the world wouldn't seem such a damn scary place all the time.

She forced herself to look away. There was nobody who could make her life better but herself. She'd figure it out, somehow.

"His vitals look good." Anson nodded at the

monitor next to the gurney. The smile that followed his words looked a little forced, as if he was trying a bit too hard to be a friend to her.

She shouldn't have dragged the poor man back here with her. He didn't really know her or Danny from Adam's house cat. "You don't have to stay with me, Mr. Daughtry."

"Anson's fine."

"Danny's going to be okay. I'm fine. We've already ruined your Friday night—"

"Ruined it?" His smile looked much more genuine this time. "I got a shiner, a busted nose and a story to tell out of it. Best Friday night ever."

She smiled. "That is so sad."

"Isn't it?" He patted the empty chair beside him. "Have a seat. I can tell you a few more sad stories that'll make your life seem like daisies and butterflies in comparison."

She sat beside him, suddenly aware of just how big a man he really was. He was lanky, yes, but not skinny. His shoulders were deliciously broad, with muscle definition even his oversize T-shirt couldn't hide. And he had a good face. A kind face, one lightly lined with creases that told her he liked to smile a lot.

She felt an entirely unexpected tug of attraction low in her belly.

"No more sad stories," She made herself look away from the melted-chocolate softness of his eyes.

"I don't know many happy ones." Though his tone remained light, she heard a melancholy note in his Tennessee drawl that caught her by surprise. For a man who so clearly liked to smile and joke, he had a streak of sadness in him. It made her heart ache.

"That's a little cynical."

"That's me." He smiled broadly, carving his smile lines deeper, and she saw what the lines had hidden—some of his smiles were all for show.

He wasn't joking, she realized. He *didn't* know many happy stories.

She suddenly felt deeply sorry for him, sorry

enough that her own considerable woes seemed lighter in comparison.

A couple of minutes later, Anson broke the tense silence that had fallen between them. "You really don't know why those men were menacing you and your brother?"

He almost sounded suspicious, she realized, though when she met his gaze, there was only kind interest there.

What might he be hiding from her behind that gentle expression?

"I have no idea, but—" She glanced at the gurney where Danny was sleeping off the booze and the injury. What she'd been on the verge of saying felt like disloyalty.

"How much do you know about what your brother does when you're not around?" Anson asked softly.

Not much, she conceded silently, taking in her brother's whipcord-lean appearance. Danny had lost a lot of weight recently. From the drinking alone? Or had he picked up other bad habits that were so easy to come by in these parts? Meth, weed, coke, smack—she knew all the recreational drugs were as readily available as home brew in the mountains. "I'm at work during the day. He goes out sometimes at night."

"Does he work?"

She shook her head. "He's a machinist. Hurt his hand about a year ago, and the doctors aren't sure how soon he'll be able to do his job again. He's drawing disability now until he's cleared to work again."

"So he has a lot of time on his hands, then."

She looked down at the tile floor of the emergency room bay, hating to hear her own worried thoughts voiced by a stranger. "He's not a bad person. When he's sober, he's so much help to me."

"How often is he sober?"

She shot him a warning look.

He pressed his mouth into a thin line and looked away.

"Maybe you *should* go," she said, hating the

tight tone of her voice, the implied ingratitude. Anson Daughtry had saved her life tonight. He'd probably saved her brother's life as well, distracting those men and sending her for help so quickly. If they'd had a few more minutes to finish the job on her brother—

"I'm sorry," Anson murmured, his baritone voice sounding like a rumble of thunder in the quiet room. "It was not my place to pry."

"No, I'm sorry." She turned to look at him. "I'm stressed out and I'm worried about Danny. I sounded so ungrateful, and I'm not, I promise you. I know what you did for Danny and me tonight." She took in his battered face, the drying blood staining his T-shirt, and her stomach knotted with sympathy. "I can see how much danger you put yourself in to help us. I just—"

"You don't have to explain." He smiled, but she didn't miss the wince in his eyes. "I'll go."

She closed her hand over his arm as he started to rise. "No. Please stay."

He settled back in the chair beside her, his

gaze meeting hers. "Addiction is awful. It just is. And addicts can be the nicest people in the world when they're clean and sober. Hell, they can be a barrel of laughs even when they're high as a kite. But they're trouble to the people who love them, no matter how hard they try not to be."

The voice of experience, she thought, her gaze shifting involuntarily toward her sleeping brother. "He's a drunk. That's the addiction I know about, anyway."

"That might be all it is."

"It's enough." She closed her eyes and leaned her head back against the wall. Beside her, she could feel the solid warmth of Anson's long, lean body. His quiet respirations helped drive away some of the gnawing fear she'd been operating under since she'd looked across the car and seen her brother's blood spilling down the front of his shirt.

Don't get too used to it, a cautionary voice whispered in her head. *He's not going to be there forever. Or even tomorrow.*

She was on her own. As always.

And she was all Danny had.

BY THE TIME the hospital in Knoxville moved Danny Coltrane to a room, midnight had come and gone. Danny had awakened during the gurney ride to the fourth floor, just sober enough to know he'd been drinking too much that night. His tearful apologies to his worried sister had grated on Anson's nerves until he was ready to explode.

Never again was the most useless phrase in the English language. It held no meaning, acted as no promise, broke a million hearts and rendered the speaker an unmitigated liar.

There was always an "again." Always.

He made his escape and waited down the hall in a small lounge area set aside for patients and families to meet without going to the formal waiting room. The area consisted of two small sofas and a handful of chairs, all empty at this hour of the early morning.

He folded himself into one of the chairs, grimacing at his own reflection in the windows. He was six foot four in his bare feet, and trying to fit his long limbs into the bowl-shaped chair he'd chosen made him look rather like a praying mantis trying to tuck itself into a walnut shell.

With a sigh, he moved to the sofa and averted his gaze from his reflection as he pulled out his phone to check his email. Twenty new messages in the past two hours. All of them virtually useless.

He rubbed his bruised rib cage, wincing at the flood of pain even his light touch evoked. He was going to be a walking bruise by morning.

He had one email from Tuck at the office. Marty Tucker was his assistant in the IT department and currently holding down the top job while Anson was on administrative leave. Anson opened the email and scanned Tuck's rambling missive about the latest glitches and grumblings from what Tuck liked to call "The Great Unwashed," those field agents at The Gates whose grasp of technology was, to be kind, subpar.

Nothing urgent or particularly interesting popped up in Tuck's verbal meanderings, though Anson was mildly amused by Tuck's latest nickname for one of their newer agents, Olivia Sharp—"Bombshell Barbie." Sharp was tall, blonde, shapely and bigger than life, and she walked around The Gates as if she owned the place. Still, she'd seemed nice enough the handful of times he'd run into her before he'd been stripped of his duties. Tuck was in mad love with her, it seemed. In that annoying way of adolescent boys.

Too bad Tuck was older than Anson.

He pocketed the phone and rose to stretch his legs, grimacing at his battered body's creaks and groans of protest. He had to keep moving—sitting still would only make the pain worse.

At least he'd have a story to tell the next time he ran into someone he knew, right? How many IT professionals could brag about taking a beating for a pretty girl?

Thinking of Ginny Coltrane brought his mood

down quickly. He'd had no idea she was living such a sad, stressful life. Sure, she didn't smile or joke much at work, but a lot of people approached work that way, with singular focus and intensity. They still had fun on the weekends or at night, enjoyed their families and friends. Anson's life was pretty solitary compared to most people's, but he had a group of old friends from high school he still spent time with on the weekends, white-water rafting or fishing or just swimming in the river where it widened and deepened down past Johnson's Dam.

He wondered if Ginny ever got the chance to slip on a bikini and spend some time on the river. Probably not. Her nights and weekends were probably spent the way she'd spent tonight—dragging her brother out of bars before he could drink himself to death.

As he neared Danny Coltrane's hospital room, he heard singing. A woman's voice—Ginny's voice—quietly singing a mournful mountain ballad he remembered from his early childhood. It was a rather gruesome lament about a woman whose love for her dead sweetheart wouldn't let him move on to his peace, but Ginny's soft alto made it sound ethereal and full of dreadful beauty.

Stopping outside the doorway, he leaned against the wall, closed his eyes and listened as she sang, remembering his mother singing the same words. His mother's voice had been warbly and slightly off-key, but he'd loved to hear her sing anyway, loved everything about her, from her rosewater scent to her soft brown hair that fell in a long braid down her back.

She'd died when he was five, leaving him alone with his father. He'd never known another moment of happiness at home.

Footsteps coming down the hall faltered, distracting him from Ginny's song. Opening his eyes, he saw a man standing about ten yards from where he stood, dressed in dark blue scrubs. But the uniform couldn't hide the shaggy beard or the hard blue eyes of the man who'd gone after Ginny tonight at the Whiskey Road Tavern.

The man with the beard locked gazes with Anson, his eyes widening.

Anson pushed away from the wall and squared himself in front of the doorway, daring the man to make a move, even though his heart was racing like a scared squirrel being chased by a hound dog.

For a second, Anson saw the man consider it. Then he turned and started running, surprisingly fast for a man his size.

Anson took off after him.

Chapter Three

The sound of running feet pounding down the corridor outside Danny's hospital room stopped Ginny's song in the middle of a verse. She turned her head in time to see Anson Daughtry speed past the open door.

With a quick glance to make sure Danny was still sleeping, she hurried out into the corridor. Down the hall, the door to the stairwell was slowly swinging shut.

The pretty dark-eyed nurse at the desk caught her eye as she passed, a frown on her face. "Friends of yours?"

Friends? As in plural? "The tall, lanky guy is. There was someone else out here?"

"An orderly, I think—at least he was wearing the uniform." She frowned. "I don't think I've ever seen him before, though. Should I call security?"

"Yes," Ginny said, heading for the stairs.

She could hear the sound of footsteps running a couple of floors below her, shoe soles squeaking on the rubber stair treads. She headed down after the sounds before she talked herself out of it. If Danny's life was in danger, she needed to know why.

On the landing two floors down, she stopped, listening for more sounds of running. Either they were so far ahead of her the sound didn't carry up to the fifth-floor landing or they'd exited on one of the floors above.

As she started back up the stairs, she heard a door swing open below and a flurry of footsteps rushing up the stairs toward her. Gripped by a sudden urge to run, she took the steps two at a time, stumbling as she reached the sixth-floor landing and hitting her shin hard on the top step.

Biting back a gasp of pain, she pushed to her feet, darting a quick look behind her.

Anson stared back at her, his eyes wide. "Are you okay?"

She slumped against the wall of the stairwell, grimacing at the throbbing ache in her bruised shin. "What the hell is going on? The nurse said you were running after some orderly?"

"We need to get back to your brother's room." The note of urgency in his voice made her stomach ache.

"Why? What happened?"

He put his hand on her shoulder, steering her toward the next set of steps. He wasn't even breathing hard, she noticed, considering he'd just gone running up and down several flights of stairs. His hand was solid but gentle against her back as he led her through the door to the seventh floor.

There was a barrel-chested black man in a security-guard uniform standing at the nurse's desk when they emerged from the stairwell. The nurse nodded toward them and the security guard started walking their way, wariness evident in his dark eyes. He kept one hand near the weapon tucked into his gun belt.

"Is there some sort of trouble?" he asked.

Anson answered in a calm, authoritative tone, "Earlier this evening, one of your patients was stabbed by one of four men who accosted him and his sister. I just spotted one of those men in a pair of scrubs heading toward his room. He turned and started running, so I went after him to see if I could catch him. But he had too large a head start, and then it occurred to me that he might have been a diversion."

Ginny looked up at Anson. "You think—" She didn't even stop to finish, darting down the hall toward her brother's room.

When she dashed into the room, she found Danny still sleeping peacefully. The monitors next to his bed showed no signs of distress.

She slumped into the chair beside his bed, pressing her face into her shaking hands.

"Is everything okay, ma'am?" The security

guard's gravelly voice made her look up. He stood in the doorway, Anson a step behind him.

"Seems to be," she answered, her voice wobblier than she liked. "I think I'd like a nurse to come check on him."

The security guard nodded and headed back down the hall.

Anson waited in the doorway, his eyes narrowed as he looked from her to Danny, then back to her. "You okay?"

She nodded. "Are you sure it was one of those guys at the Whiskey Road?"

He entered the room, nodding. "Why would they come all the way here to go after him again?"

"I have no idea," she admitted, feeling scared and helpless. It was a terrible feeling, one she'd experienced far too many times growing up, and she struggled not to give in. "I honestly don't. Danny hasn't said anything about being in trouble, and I haven't noticed anyone suspicious hanging around the property or anything—"

"Does he live with you?"

"Since he went on disability."

A nurse entered then, smiling at Ginny as she crossed to take a look at the monitor by Danny's bed. "All his vitals look good."

Danny stirred at the sound of the nurse's voice, his eyes squinting at the light overhead. "Whass 'appenin'?

Ginny rose to comfort him. "Nothing's happening, Danny. Why don't you go back to sleep? You'll feel a lot better in the morning."

His eyes stopped struggling to focus and within a minute, he was asleep again. Ginny stared down at him, torn between wanting to tuck him in and wanting to jerk him up by the hair and shake him for what he was putting her through these days.

"He seems to be recovering nicely," the nurse said with a gentle smile. "Call us if you need us."

Ginny moved away from the hospital bed and sat down again, slumping forward, her forearms resting on her knees.

"You're going to stay here all night, aren't you?" Anson asked.

She looked up at him. "Yeah."

"Did you call Quinn?"

She shook her head, feeling defeated. She had so much work on her desk waiting to be processed, and now she'd be another day behind. "I'll call in the morning. I guess I'll need to ask for a few days off."

"No," Anson said.

She looked up at him. "No?"

"There's no reason for you to stay here with your brother for three days while he detoxes. You're not his mother."

Anger at his presumption flooded her tense gut as she rose to her feet. "You don't have a say in what I do or don't do."

"No, I don't. But I do have experience with drunks. And there's no way you can baby him back to health. He has to want it for himself." There was no hardness in Anson's words, no censure. His rumbly voice was gentle and even sympathetic. "Until he wants it for himself, you're just standing in the way of a freight train that has no intention of putting on the brakes."

"I don't think my staying here is going to make him stop drinking," she said in a softer tone. "But if you're right about that orderly being one of the men from the bar, then he might be in danger."

"And you think you're big enough to stop one of those guys?"

"No. But if I'm here, I can call for help."

He looked as if he wanted to argue. But finally, he gave a brief nod. "Fair enough. But you're going to need to sleep sometimes. You can't stay here playing bodyguard around the clock."

"There's no one else to do it." She sat in the chair again, wrapping her arms around her stomach, hoping to calm a sudden case of the shakes. She was starting to feel completely overwhelmed.

"Yes, there is," Anson said quietly. "I can stay with your brother."

She looked up again to see if he was serious. He was. She shook her head quickly. "No, that's—I mean, it's very nice of you to offer—"

"Thanks but no thanks?"

"Mr. Daughtry—"

"Anson," he corrected gently.

"It's a generous offer, but you don't really know us. And I don't really know you that well, and Danny doesn't know you at all. And surely you have other things to do with your time."

"Right now? Not so much." He looked around the room, spotted a second chair and crossed to bring it closer to the recliner where she sat. He leaned forward until his eyes were level with hers. "I have an ulterior motive. I'll admit that."

"What's that?"

"I'm bored. I don't have a job to go to, and I don't have anything interesting set up on the side while I'm waiting for Quinn and his investigators to finally figure out I'm not out there leaking company secrets like a rusty pipe. Plus, I happen to have a little experience with people who drink too much. And maybe it's a good thing Danny doesn't know me, you know?"

"You think I'm a pushover."

"Didn't say that."

"Didn't have to." She looked over at her brother. He was still asleep, his face soft and boyish, reminding her of the boy he'd once been. She sighed. "I know I'm too soft on him. But he's all I have."

"Believe me, I get that." A melancholy note in Anson's deep voice drew her attention back to him. He was looking at her, his gaze warm and serious. "I know what it's like to be you. Only it was my father. And he never recovered."

The thought of losing Danny to booze or, God forbid, drugs was enough to send a chill all the way to her bone marrow. She hugged herself more tightly. "I'm sorry."

"Let me do this. I'll even stay tonight if you want so you can go home and get some sleep."

She shook her head. "No car, remember?"

"Oh, right."

As an awkward silence descended between them, there was a light knock on the door, and a moment later, the security guard who'd questioned them earlier stuck his head through the doorway. "Everything okay in here?"

"Yes, thank you," she said, managing a weak smile at the man.

"Did you find the man with the beard?" Anson asked.

The security guard shook his head. "He could have gotten out of the hospital before we even got a chance to start looking. I've alerted the guards to keep an eye out for him, and I'll be staying on this floor for the night, just in case."

"Thank you."

Anson turned to look at her after the security guard closed the door behind him. "I don't think they'll try anything again tonight."

"I hope you're right."

He pushed to his feet. "I'm going to head on out and leave you and your brother alone. Is there anything I can do for you before I go?"

She shook her head. "I'm good."

He looked at Danny. "He might want some clothes for tomorrow. A change of underwear or something. You may want some clean clothes, too. Is there someone I can call to get some things for y'all?"

She hated to admit there was no one, but it was the truth. She worked all the time, and Danny's drinking had made it hard for them to do any sort of socializing with their neighbors. "No. Maybe I can run home sometime tomorrow and grab a few things—"

"No car," he reminded her.

Her heart sank. "Right."

"I can do it for you. If you trust me."

She stared at him for a moment, suddenly uncertain. He had been a lifesaver for her that night—literally. But what did she really know about Anson Daughtry? If the people she worked with at The Gates were telling the truth, Anson was a free spirit who looked like a redneck and thought like a tech genius. But he was also on administrative leave from the company, the prime suspect in a case of industrial espionage.

Nobody at The Gates seemed to believe he was guilty, though—

"Forget I suggested it." Anson turned to go.

She caught his hand, holding him in place. "Wait."

He looked down at her fingers closed around his. His hand was warm and rougher than she expected, more like a workman's hand than that of a man who worked on computers all day long.

His gaze swept up to meet hers, dark and soft. "Yes?"

"I would really appreciate it if you would get a few things for Danny and me," she said, releasing his hand. Her fingers still tingled a little where their skin had touched.

Shoving his hands into the pockets of his jeans, he nodded. "Okay."

She grabbed her purse from the floor and pulled out her keys to remove the house key from the ring. "Here's the key to the house. The driveway circles around to the back—you can park there. The back door opens to the kitchen. Just go through there to the hall. My room is on the right. Danny's is on the left."

"You want me to pick out some things for you, too?" he asked with a slow smile that made her own lips curve in response. "Go through your unmentionables? You're a brave woman, Ginny Coltrane."

"Or crazy," she murmured. "Clean jeans and a T-shirt for me. A change of underwear. Think you can handle that?"

"I think I'll manage. What about your brother? He have any jogging shorts, something like that?"

"I think he does. That sounds perfect. Thank you." She told him her address and he jotted it down on his phone. "I really appreciate this."

"Give me your phone number and I'll call if I have trouble finding anything."

She told him her cell-phone number and he typed that into his phone, as well. "Are you going tonight or in the morning?"

"I was thinking maybe tonight," he answered. "You're probably going to be awake for a little while longer, right?"

She nodded. "I'm not sure how easy it'll be to fall asleep tonight."

"I'll go now, then. And if I need your help finding anything, I'll call you. Sound like a deal?"

"Sounds like a deal," she agreed.

He left the room with a little wave of one large hand, closing the door behind him.

Ginny looked around the quiet hospital room, feeling as scared and alone as she'd felt in a long, long time.

GINNY COLTRANE'S SMALL bungalow sat in the heart of Two Souls Hollow, a small valley cut through the mountains north of Purgatory. The homes in this part of the hollow were spaced far enough apart that Anson couldn't see either of the neighbors' homes from the car park behind the house.

It wasn't the kind of house paid for by corporate

espionage, he thought with a frown. Not that he'd been thinking of her as a suspect for the past few hours, not since she turned those big blue eyes on him and transformed him into a love-struck adolescent.

Where was Danny's car? he wondered as he parked in the empty drive behind the house. If it had been parked at the Whiskey Road Tavern, surely Ginny would have taken it to the hospital rather than depending on him for a ride. If there was something he was beginning to realize about her, it was that she liked to handle things on her own whenever possible.

She lived in a small town, but there were no neighbors she trusted to pick up a few things for her stay. She had no family to speak of, besides her alcoholic brother. He'd never seen her socializing with anyone at the office, either—she had a work ethic that would put most CEOs to shame.

What did she do for fun?

Did she ever get to have any fun?

"Now I'm depressing myself," he muttered as

he pulled out the house key Ginny had lent him and unlocked the back door.

The light switch was just inside the door. He flicked it on and took a quick look around the small, neat kitchen. The house wasn't new, and neither were the appliances, but everything seemed to be clean and well maintained. There were dishes drying on the rack by the sink and a neatly folded dish towel on the counter, the only sign that the kitchen had been used that day.

He went through the door into the hallway and took a left into Danny's bedroom. It wasn't nearly as neat as the kitchen, though he wouldn't show up on any reality show about hoarders or anything. His bed was unmade, the pillows lying haphazardly across the mattress. There was an empty glass on the nightstand, as well. Anson took a sniff, surprised that he couldn't smell any alcohol. Maybe he didn't do any drinking around the house?

Yeah, no. Alcoholics always had a stash. Always.

Anson found Danny's in the sock drawer of his chest of drawers, tucked near the back of the drawer. Two bottles of Jack Daniel's, only one full. The other was half-gone.

He left them there, though he would tell Ginny the next time he talked to her so she could get rid of it before Danny returned home.

But his next discovery caught him off guard. In the underwear drawer, wrapped up in a pair of boxer shorts, he found a bag of white powder. Short of dipping his finger into the bag and tasting it—which sounded like a really stupid idea—he could only assume it was some sort of illicit substance. Or why would Danny have bothered to hide it in his underwear drawer?

Hating to do it, he pulled out his phone and dialed Ginny's cell phone.

She answered on the first ring. "Hello?"

"Ginny, it's Anson Daughtry. I'm at your place, picking up the change of clothes and I found something in one of Danny's drawers."

"He has a stash of booze there, doesn't he?"

"Yes, but that's not the only thing." He told her about the plastic bag containing the white powder.

She was silent for so long he wondered if the call had been cut off. Just before he spoke, she said, "Can you tell what it is?"

"Probably coke or heroin," he said. "Meth usually comes in crystalized form. Have you ever known him to do drugs?"

"No," she said with a weary sigh. "But it's not like drugs are hard to find in these damn hills."

"The hospital may have done a tox screen on Danny in the ER. I don't suppose he's put your name on his medical forms to have information released to you, has he?"

"I honestly don't know." She sounded bone-tired and utterly devastated. Anson wished he could reach through the phone and give her an encouraging hug, a feeling that should have alarmed him but somehow didn't.

"I think we need to dispose of it, whatever it

is. There's enough here to get your brother in a mess if the police were to conduct a raid."

"Maybe I should turn him in."

The pain in her voice made his chest ache. "Do you think that would help him? Or do you think it would just make him cut you out of his life completely?"

"I don't know." She was crying now, damn it. He'd made her cry.

"Listen, I'm going to get rid of this stuff. Flush it down the toilet and put the bag in the trash. You hang in there and I'll be back at the hospital before you know it." He pulled out the clothing he'd come there to gather for Danny. "Does Danny have a gym bag or something I could put the clothes in?"

"In his closet," she directed. "It's the door to your right if you're facing the chest of drawers."

He opened the closet, wary about what he'd find inside. But it was an ordinary storage space, with a few clothes hanging from the bar at the top and several pairs of shoes lined up on the floor next to a dark blue gym bag.

The bag was empty, so Anson stuffed Danny's clothes inside. "Your room next. Any drawers you want me to avoid?"

"You're a big boy. I think you can handle anything in my drawers." She made a watery sound that might have been a laugh. "Wait. That sounded really naughty."

He laughed as he crossed to her bedroom and flicked on the light. It was neater than Danny's room, but it still had a slightly messy, lived-in feel he rather liked. No flowers or knickknacks, no candles or fluffy throw pillows in this room, just a four-poster bed covered with a handmade quilt and two pillows in white cases. "Nice room."

"Thanks. Did I remember to make the bed?"

"You did." He crossed to the tall chest of drawers beside the bed. "I'm at the chest of drawers. What do you want from what drawer?"

"The top drawer is my underwear. A couple of panties and bras would be great."

He opened the drawer and found panties and bras inside, neatly folded. Pretty, bright colors, he saw, but none of the bras seemed to go with any of the panties. "Do you care if they match?"

"No," she answered. After a few seconds, she added, "This is such a strange conversation."

"I like to think of it as getting to know you, kamikaze-style." He grabbed a couple of sets of underwear and put them in the bag. "What else?"

As she started to speak, he heard the sound of shattering glass coming from somewhere in the house.

It was apparently loud enough to carry through the phone, for a second later, Ginny asked, "What was that?"

"I'm not sure," he answered, keeping his voice low. He stepped out of her room into the hall. From there, he could see into the kitchen. Nothing seemed out of place.

Then he heard the sound of more glass breaking, coming from the front of the house. Glass clattered onto a hard surface, then a second later came the unmistakable crunch of glass being broken underfoot.

"Anson?" Ginny's voice rose in his ear.

He ducked back into her bedroom and eased the door closed, his heart pounding. "Someone's breaking into your house."

Chapter Four

"Someone is what?"

Next to Ginny, Danny stirred in his sleep, making a low, groaning noise as the movement apparently pulled at the stitches in his side. She got up and moved toward the door, straining to hear Anson's whispered response.

"Someone's breaking into your house. I'm in your bedroom and I don't think I can make it to the back door without drawing their attention."

"Get off the phone with me and call 9-1-1."

"I'm holding at least five ounces of what is almost certainly an illegal drug. The cops will want to know why."

She glanced back at Danny, scowling. Damn

it. "There's no great place to hide there. It's not a big house."

"I'm aware of that," he muttered. "No attic? Maybe there's a trapdoor in the top of your closet?"

"There's an attic, but it's little more than a crawl space. And the trapdoor is out in the hall."

"Yeah, that won't work."

"The windows in my room are painted shut, but there's a window that opens in the bathroom. It's the next room down across from my bedroom. Do you think you can get there?"

"Not sure," he admitted. "Give me a sec." She heard the muffled sound of breathing, the rustle of fabric against the microphone. He must have the phone pressed against his shirt, she guessed, frustrated by trying to figure out what was going on with nothing but her ears to work with.

A moment later, he whispered into the phone again. "I'm in the bathroom. I've closed and locked the door, but I'm not sure if they heard me. I may not have a lot of time."

"They?" she asked softly, her heart in her throat.

"At least two. I heard them talking when I crossed the hall."

Damn it. The window in the bathroom might open, but it wasn't quiet about it. "Anson, the bathroom window creaks when you open it. Kind of loudly. They'll hear you."

He muttered a soft profanity. "Okay, any other ideas?"

She pressed her forehead against the hospital room door, feeling like an idiot. She should have thought about the noise before she ran him into the bathroom with no way to escape. "Flush the drugs and call 9-1-1," she said. "Then get in the tub and back up closest to the faucets. There's not a good angle to that part of the tub through the door, so even if they start shooting, they're not going to hit you."

"That lock isn't going to withstand a couple of good kicks."

"I don't know!" Her voice rose, and once again Danny stirred in the hospital bed. "I don't know," she repeated in a hushed tone. "I don't know what you should do."

"Yes, you do," he said a second later, his voice a low growl. "Call Quinn."

"At this hour?"

"Yes, at this hour. You have anything to write with?"

She looked around stupidly for a moment, her mind reeling. Then she saw her purse and rushed over to it, digging in one of the pockets for a notepad she kept there. "Okay."

He rattled off a phone number. "That's Quinn's personal cell. Tell him where I am. Tell him there's trouble and I need assistance immediately. And don't worry if he snarls at you. He always snarls when you call at this time of night."

That was reassuring. "Okay, got it. Give me five minutes, then call me back."

"Might be a little busy."

"Call me back if you can," she insisted, her pulse thudding heavily in her throat. "Please."

"Call Quinn," he said quickly and hung up.

She punched in the number he'd given her, her hands shaking. Lifting the phone to her ear, she slumped in the recliner beside Danny's bed and waited for someone to answer.

It took four rings before a slow, drawling voice answered. "Marbury Motors twenty-four-hour hotline."

Had she dialed the wrong number? "Um, is Mr. Quinn there?"

For a second, there was nothing but silence. Then she heard the familiar rumble of Alexander Quinn's voice. "Where did you get this number, Ms. Coltrane?"

"Anson Daughtry," she answered, nearly fainting with relief. "He's in trouble."

THE WHITE POWDER spread across the toilet water and began to dissolve more quickly than Anson had expected. He'd figured if it were cocaine, as he suspected, it might be cut with something that would make it harder for the powder to dissolve, but what he was looking at was apparently high-grade coke. Only a small amount of residue remained in the bottom of the toilet bowl after he emptied the bag into the bowl.

On the chance that the men he could hear moving around outside the bathroom door decided to kick down the door before Quinn could send reinforcements, Anson climbed into the built-in tub as Ginny had suggested.

He'd barely flattened himself to the wall under the shower faucet when he heard the doorknob rattle.

"Locked," he heard a male voice mutter. A second voice answered with a vulgar epithet.

"We'll come back to it," the first voice said, and Anson heard footsteps moving away from the bathroom door.

He closed his eyes and released a long, quiet breath as he pulled the phone from his pocket and checked the time. Five minutes had come and gone. He hadn't actually promised Ginny he'd call, but the thought of her sitting there worrying about him on top of all the stress already pressing down on her was more than he could stand.

He dialed her number. She answered on the first ring. "Anson?"

"Did you get Quinn?" he whispered.

"Yes. He said to tell you he was on the way with reinforcements."

Anson laid his head back against the tub wall. "Thank you. Did he give you any trouble?"

"You forgot to tell me there was some sort of code involved. I thought he was going to hang up on me."

"Sorry." He'd forgotten about the code himself. "How's Danny? Still hanging in there okay?"

She was silent for a long moment before she finally spoke. "You're worrying about Danny at a time like this?"

"Just trying to distract myself from the men wandering around outside the bathroom, biding their time before they decide to bust down the door and shoot my trouble-prone ass."

"Danny's fine," she answered tightly. "Please don't let anybody shoot you, okay?"

"Worried about me?"

"Thinking about how hard it is to get blood out of tile grout," she answered bluntly.

He bit back surprised laughter. "You're a hard-hearted woman."

"It's hard keeping a nice house, working as many hours as I do." Her voice softened. "And I'm worried about you."

"They're leaving the bathroom for later," he told her. "I don't think they suspect yet that any-one is here."

"What if they see your car?"

"Maybe they'll think it's Danny's."

"Danny doesn't have a car. His license got sus-pended last year for a DUI. He's not allowed to drive. Everybody who knows him knows that. He sold his car to pay the fines."

Good God, Anson thought. Ginny was either a saint or a fool to put up with a brother like that. "If they start to get serious about coming in here,

I'm going out the window," he told her. "I think I'll have enough of a head start to beat them outside, but I'm not sure I can get to my car."

"The woods are deep. Head east and you'll hit the main highway back to Purgatory."

A moment later, he heard the doorknob rattle again. His cue, he thought. "I'm going out the window."

"Be careful!" Her voice rang with worry.

He hung up, shoved his phone into his pocket and climbed out of the tub, not bothering with stealth. He flipped the lock and gave the window a hard upward shove. It slid open with a loud creak, making him wince.

Climbing onto the toilet seat, he pushed himself out the window headfirst, twisting as he went. He hit hard on the ground below, landing on his knees. A sharp rock dug into the flesh of his right shin, eliciting a soft curse. Then he was up and running, ignoring the pains shooting through his battered body like bolts of lightning racing across a stormy sky.

As he neared the corner of the house, he heard the back door opening, the screen door creaking.

Reversing direction, he bolted toward the woods, hoping he was heading east. He heard a bark of gunfire behind him, but the bullet thudded into a tree several feet away. Still, he zigzagged as he ran, not wanting to present an easy target.

Suddenly, he heard the unmistakable click of a rifle bolt being shoved into position. He froze in place, his heart rattling wildly in his chest.

"Daughtry."

He turned slowly and found himself looking at a tall, black-clad figure holding a large, terrifying-looking rifle. It took him a moment to look beyond the rifle barrel to see familiar eyes glittering in the waning moonlight.

"Brand," he breathed, his knees shaky as he recognized one of Quinn's top agents.

"What's the situation?" Adam Brand asked, sounding like the FBI agent he used to be.

"I was getting some clothes for Ginny Coltrane—long story," he added at the sight of Brand's quirked eyebrows. "While I was there, I heard someone break into the house through the front windows. I was on the phone with Ginny and had her call Quinn."

Brand nodded, his eyes narrowing. "Why Quinn and not the police?"

Yeah, Anson thought, suddenly feeling stupid. *Why Quinn and not the police, again? Oh, yeah, because you dumped several ounces of illegal coke down the toilet and didn't want the cops to find out.*

"I didn't want the local yokels to mistake me for one of the intruders," he answered, hoping that would be answer enough.

"My wife is one of the local yokels," Brand said bluntly.

Well, hell. So she is. "Not her jurisdiction, though."

"I wouldn't use that excuse with Dennison," Brand warned, motioning for Anson to follow him deeper into the woods. "This *is* his fiancée's jurisdiction."

"Right." What was it about The Gates agents and their fetish for women in uniform, anyway? "Is there a team going into the house?"

"Not my assignment," Brand said, starting to pull ahead. Grimacing against the lingering ache in his battered limbs, Anson hurried to catch up.

"You'll have to take stock to tell us if anything is missing." Alexander Quinn's voice was a reassuring rumble on the other end of the call. "The intruders were gone when the team I sent entered the house. I guess Daughtry spooked them and they left."

Ginny leaned her head back against the recliner, the adrenaline that had kept her going for the past few hours starting to drain, leaving only bone-deep weariness in its wake. "And Anson's okay?"

"He says he's fine." Quinn's voice dipped lower.

"He looks like hell, though. I understand he took a beating tonight?"

She closed her eyes, remembering the sight of Anson's battered face. "He took a beating for my brother and me."

"He also tried to hide evidence for you," Quinn said flatly.

"It was my idea," she said. "I asked him to do it."

"I'm not judging," Quinn said in a tone that suggested otherwise. "I didn't realize you and Daughtry were close."

Whoa, she thought. Quinn made it sound like—

"We're not really close. He was just kind enough to help me out tonight."

"Took a beating, hid evidence, dodged bullets—"

She sat up straight. "Bullets? He dodged bullets?"

"Did you think you were dealing with jaywalkers?"

"I don't know who I'm dealing with," she admitted, feeling sick. "Or why I'm dealing with them."

"You're a smart woman. Hazard a guess." Quinn hung up before she could respond.

She hung up the phone and turned to look at Danny sleeping soundly in the hospital bed beside her. She'd thought things were bad enough when all she was dealing with was alcohol. At least alcohol was legal.

But drugs, too?

There was a light knock on the door. She looked up, expecting the night nurse. Instead, it was Anson who entered the room, carrying Danny's gym bag.

"What are you doing back here?" she asked. "You should be home in bed."

"Couldn't sleep." He picked up the extra chair and set it down next to the recliner. Dropping into the seat, he turned to look at her. "Brought y'all a change of clothes. And I figured while I was here, I'd spell you so you could get some rest."

"Like I could sleep."

"You should try. The next three days are going to be long."

She knew he was right, but Quinn's call had reignited her adrenaline flow. "Quinn said the intruders shot at you."

"They missed me," he said lightly, but he couldn't hide the tense set of his broad shoulders or the knotting muscles in his jaw.

"You should never have been a target. Not for Danny and me." She shook her head, guilt swamping her. "Go home. This isn't your problem."

"They beat me up and shot at me. It's my problem now."

"Not if you go home and forget about it. You have enough to worry about, with the suspension and trying to clear your name."

Anson's facial expression shifted a little, though she couldn't quite make out what emotion passed across his features before he lifted his calm gaze to meet hers. His dark eyes were mirrors, reflecting back only her own taut expression of worry.

"I've just about exhausted all the ideas I had for proving I'm not leaking agency secrets. I could use the distraction."

"Dodging bullets isn't a distraction."

"*Dodging* is overstating things. The guy was a lousy shot."

"Don't joke about it! Do you know how horrible I would feel if something happened to you because you were trying to help me?"

He covered her hand with his, his fingers warm and strong. "It didn't. I'm fine."

She couldn't stop herself from turning her palm up to clasp his hand. "Quinn knows you were trying to destroy the drugs."

"Yeah. I didn't get a chance to flush before he and the others got to the house." He looked down at their clasped hands, his expression softening. "Sorry about that."

"Don't apologize. I should never have put you in that position."

"It got flushed, in the end. And Quinn took the bag with him. I think he's planning to have the lab at The Gates test it so you'll know what you're dealing with."

She let go of his hand, wrapping her arms around her aching stomach. "There's no way he's going to want me to come back to The Gates after this."

"Of course he will."

He sounded awfully confident for someone who was on administrative leave himself, she thought. "I don't even know how to deal with Danny's drinking. If he's doing drugs now, too—"

"Yeah, about that." Anson leaned forward, resting his elbows on his knees. He looked down at the hospital room's drab tile floor, his jaw muscles working for a few seconds before he spoke again. "I talked to our drug-interdiction expert at The Gates, Caleb Cooper."

She tried to match the name to a face. Cooper was a relatively new hire, wasn't he? Rusty-haired, freckled, laughed a lot. "I didn't realize we had a drug-interdiction expert."

"Quinn thought it would be prudent to have

someone on staff who had some experience with the drug trade. Cooper worked at the Birmingham Police Department on their drug-interdiction task force before he hired on with The Gates. Anyway, he said that the amount of drugs I flushed wasn't likely to be someone's personal stash. There was too much."

"How much was there?"

"Over a hundred grams. Probably more."

She closed her eyes. She certainly wasn't an expert on illegal drugs, but that many grams sounded like something a whole lot worse than a drug problem. "Cooper thinks Danny is dealing?"

"Maybe dealing. Maybe transporting. Someone could be using him as their mule."

"He doesn't even have a car. How's he supposed to be any sort of drug transporter?"

"I think that's a question we need to ask Danny when he's sober and awake enough to answer." Anson turned his head to look at her. "Do you think he'll tell you the truth?"

She honestly didn't know. She and Danny had always been close, had built a relationship of mutual support thanks to an absent father— or fathers—and an irresponsible, undependable mother. But their mother's death had hit them both hard, and in some ways, Danny had grown away from her afterward. He'd hid his drinking habit for months. And she hadn't had any inkling that he was mixed up in drugs.

"We can worry about that tomorrow." Anson's tone was so gentle it brought tears to her eyes. She blinked them away, angry at herself for the sign of weakness. She couldn't afford to be soft anymore. She couldn't afford vulnerability, not if she was going to have to fight for Danny's life.

"You should go home," she said, lifting her chin and making herself meet the concern in his dark eyes. "I'm fine."

"I know you're fine. And I'm not going home, but if you want me to make myself scarce, I can go down the hall to wait." He started to get up.

She caught his hand. "Stay."

He sat again, holding on to her hand. "It's okay to need a little help."

She tugged her hand away, softening the retreat with a smile. "Well, if you're sticking around, don't suppose you have a deck of cards on you?"

"As a matter of fact—" He reached into the duffel bag and pulled out a familiar-looking box. "I found it in your bedroom when I finished packing clothes for you. It looked well-worn, so I figured you might like to have something to pass the time." He grinned at her as he handed over the cards. The expression carved deep, sexy lines into his lean face and she had to drag her gaze away before she started swooning like a groupie at a rock concert.

She closed her hands around the box of cards. "Thank you."

"We could play strip poker."

She slanted a look at him. The wicked gleam in his eyes sent a little earthquake through her insides. "I sent you to bring me more clothes, not strip me of the ones I'm wearing."

"As exciting as that sounds, I'm a terrible card-player. I'd be down to my skivvies in no time."

"As exciting as *that* sounds," she countered with a reluctant grin, "my game is Solitaire."

He made a face, clapping his hand to his heart. "Ouch."

"Although—ever played Slapjack?"

He arched an eyebrow at her. "You have a violent streak, do you?"

"Purgatory Elementary School Slapjack champion, five years running." She opened the box of cards and pulled out the deck. Shuffling the cards with the ease that came from years of practice, she watched Anson's face for his reaction.

He watched her fingers fly, a hint of surprised admiration in his expression. "You sure you're not a cardsharp? 'Cause I'm not ashamed of my body if you want to rethink the strip poker—"

Before she could come up with a suitably smart-ass reply, her cell phone rang. She pulled it from her jeans pocket and looked at the display. The caller's identity was blocked, just as it had been when Quinn had called her earlier.

"Quinn?" Anson asked.

"Probably." She answered. "Hello?"

The voice on the other line was unfamiliar and as hard as mountain granite. "When your brother sobers up, give him a message for me."

"Who is this?" Her voice came out low and strangled. Anson's eyes snapped up to meet hers, his expression instantly alert.

"Tell your brother he's a dead man."

"Wait—"

But the line had gone dead.

Chapter Five

Ginny looked exhausted. She never wore a lot of makeup to begin with, and what little she'd been wearing when she went to the Whiskey Road Tavern to fetch her drunk brother had been worn off by worry and time. Her blue eyes were enormous in her pale face, dark circles bruising the skin around them. Her lips were bloodless except for the little piece of lower lip she kept worrying with her small white teeth as Alexander Quinn and a handful of agents moved around her, taking charge of her brother's security.

And somehow, Anson realized with no small measure of dismay, she still managed to look like sunshine and rainbows and everything that was good about the world.

"I can't pay for this," Ginny said quietly to no one in particular, finally meeting Anson's gaze with a look of sheer panic. "I don't have the money to pay for this."

"Quinn doesn't expect you to," he reassured her, taking her hand and leading her from the hospital, out of the agents' way. "After he came to my rescue at your place, he went to Whiskey Road to see if Jase has any security cameras installed. Turns out, he does."

"So they got pictures of the men who attacked Danny?" Her eyes widened with excitement, the first hint of color washing back into her face.

"They didn't catch the stabbing on video. Your car was parked at the wrong angle for the cameras to catch any images. But they did record the attack on me, and Quinn apparently recognized at least one of the guys as Ferris Bellander. Top lieutenant with the Tennessee branch of the Blue Ridge Infantry."

"Those guys are with the BRI?" She frowned. "That doesn't make any sense. Does it?"

"I didn't think it did, either," Anson admitted. "But apparently there've been signs that the BRI has dropped any pretense that they're anything but a criminal enterprise. Seems they think the local drug trade is more lucrative than marching around pretending to be an army of sovereign citizens."

"Most of the local trade is pot and meth, though. Right?" She lowered her voice, glancing around the hospital corridor. "But that stuff you found in Danny's drawer wasn't either of those things."

"They may be branching out into stuff coming up from South America."

"Coke."

"Heroin, too. Higher-end stuff."

"This is not the area to try to sell the high-end stuff," she said with a grimace. "With all the poverty around these parts—"

"Maybe it's not about selling the drugs around here. Maybe it's about distribution to other areas."

"We're not exactly a transportation hub here in Ridge County."

"No, but there are a hell of a lot of places around here where you can hide big stashes of illegal drugs for months without anyone finding them."

"So we're the warehouse?"

"Purgatory is less than twenty miles from Knoxville. Easy drive. And from Knoxville, you can hit an interstate going to Kentucky, Virginia, Western Tennessee, Georgia, South Carolina, Alabama—"

"Once you get on the interstate system, you can go almost anywhere."

He nodded. "When I talked to Quinn about Bellander and the drugs, he admitted he's been expecting something like this to come up. Some sort of distribution scheme. The BRI has been working hard to keep the organization from fracturing from all the infighting, and Quinn figured there was a reason why they wanted to stay connected rather than branching off into smaller cells."

"So much for their patriotism."

"Never had any of that," Anson answered flatly. He had a "don't tread on me" streak himself, so he could sympathize with people who viewed a large, centralized federal government with a healthy dose of skepticism. But what the Blue Ridge Infantry was doing these days had nothing to do with constitutional rights and freedoms. They were straight-up thugs, and he wanted to be part of taking them down.

Instead, here he was, stuck on the sidelines watching it happen without his help.

The soft squeeze of Ginny's fingers around his reminded him that he was still holding her hand. It had felt so right, he'd forgotten to let go.

He released her hand, earning a slight frown from her that made his heart do a little flip. "What?" he asked.

"I just wanted to thank you again. I really don't

know what I'd have done if you hadn't been there at the tavern. Or here when that call came in."

He looked down at his feet, feeling like a liar. Would she be as grateful had she known he'd been at the Whiskey Road Tavern because he was following her? Would she look at him so sweetly if she'd known she was his prime suspect for the information leaks at The Gates?

Was she still his prime suspect, now that he knew her a little better?

He didn't want to believe it, but what did he really know about her?

"You don't have to thank me," he murmured, swallowing the guilt.

"I don't have a lot of friends," she said after a moment of thick silence. "Letting other people help me out—it's not something that comes easily to me. If I've seemed at all ungrateful—"

"You haven't."

"How many people does Quinn plan to station here?" she asked, glancing back at the door of her brother's hospital room.

"He said two." He put his hand on her arm, giving a light tug to draw her farther away from the room, and lowered his voice. "Quinn's also supplying Danny with legal counsel for when the police come in the morning to question him."

Her eyes widened with alarm. "You think he could be arrested?"

"I think Quinn wants to make sure he's not. But he also wants Caleb Cooper to talk to Danny, see if we can get to the bottom of what he was doing with that bag of white powder."

"How long will it take to find out what was in the bag?"

"Quinn said he got the lab techs out of bed and put a rush job on it."

Ginny shot him a look of consternation. "Why is Mr. Quinn doing this? This is a whole lot of trouble to go to for an ordinary administrative assistant—"

He bent closer. "Ginny, Quinn doesn't hire ordinary people. Believe me, when he decided to hire you, it was because he saw something in you that he thought would be a long-term, valuable asset to The Gates."

He saw a flicker of pleasure pass across her expression and realized, with dismay, that she had no idea that someone might consider her worth knowing and defending. Even he, in his most morose moments, never doubted that he had something to contribute to the world around him. Not even his father could convince him otherwise.

"So he's protecting his asset?"

"You're part of the team now. Quinn and everybody else at The Gates is going to have your back. So just try to relax and let them help you out." He put his finger under her chin, tipping her head up until her gaze met his. She looked so tired, so careworn, it made his heart hurt. "You need to get some sleep. You're not going to be any good to your brother if you're dragging around half-dead."

"I'm good for a little longer—"

"No, you're not. Why don't we see about getting you a hotel room here in town so you can get a little sleep—"

"No," she said quickly. "I don't want to stay in a hotel room alone. I just—" She rubbed her arms as if she was chilled. "I know I should be a big girl, but I don't want to be alone right now."

"Then come home with me," he said without thinking.

ALEXANDER QUINN STEPPED off the elevator on the fifth floor of Westridge Medical Center and immediately spotted Anson Daughtry standing in the corridor with Ginny Coltrane. He ignored them for the moment and started toward Adam Brand, who was standing guard outside a closed door.

Brand nodded in greeting. "Figured you'd show sooner or later."

"Cooper inside with Danny Coltrane?"

"As you asked."

Quinn glanced down the hall at Daughtry and Ginny. "How is she?"

"I didn't get a chance to speak to her yet. Daughtry pulled her aside a few minutes ago and has been talking to her ever since." Brand gave a little shrug. "She seems overwhelmed."

Quinn imagined she was. From the extraction team's report on what Daughtry told them about the events of the evening, the woman had been through a double dose of stress. While he knew she was stronger than she looked—stronger than even she knew—she had to be worried and tired and ready to drop.

She wouldn't, though. He'd seen her backbone too many times to think she'd ever stop fighting. It was a quality he'd seen in her from the first day she stepped into his office to apply for a job.

He had a feeling she was going to need every ounce of that fighting spirit she could muster over the coming days.

"You think this is proof of your theory about the BRI's shift in focus, don't you?" Brand asked softly.

Quinn looked up at him. "Don't you?"

"I'm trying not to jump to conclusions. But yeah. I do."

"Well, at least this sort of crime is more clearly actionable." Quinn sighed. "Being a militia isn't illegal in this country for the time being, and I'm in no hurry to deny people their constitutional rights to bear arms and freely assemble."

"If that was all the BRI were doing, nobody would give a damn about them," Brand said flatly. "But you know better than anyone that's not all they've been doing."

"I'm going to talk to hospital security to see if there's a possibility they've captured the intruder on video. If so, we need to make sure the evidence is protected. We may need every ounce of proof we can get our hands on to build a RICO Act case against the BRI. Drug charges won't be enough—we need to prove a wide-reaching criminal conspiracy." While Quinn wasn't a fan of the wide ranging scope of the Racketeer Influenced and Corrupt Organization Act, it was made for criminal organizations like the BRI.

"When are we going to bring in the authorities?" Brand asked.

Quinn slanted a hard look at Brand. "When there's too much evidence for someone to sweep under the rug."

Brand grimaced but didn't respond. Brand's wife was a local cop with the Bitterwood Police Department, which had recently overhauled nearly the entire force to root out and destroy the corruption from within. He knew how bad things could be on some of the small, insular police forces in the mountain towns of Appalachia. "What about Ginny Coltrane and her brother? They could be in serious danger."

Quinn glanced down the hall, where Ginny and Anson Daughtry were deep in conversation. "Maybe it'll give Daughtry something to do with his time besides playing video games and following punk bands around the South."

Brand laughed softly. "Still nothing new on the leaks investigation?"

Quinn shook his head, his own smile fading.

"It's not Daughtry. I'm sure of that. But I'm beginning to think he may be the one who can lead us to the mole."

"You think he knows who it is?"

"I think he has the information needed to figure it out," Quinn said with a shake of his head. "I'm just trying to motivate him to put his genius to work so he can save his own ass."

"GO HOME WITH YOU?" Even as she repeated Anson's words, Ginny knew she sounded dull-witted and slow.

"I have a big place in Purgatory." He sounded uncertain, and she wondered if he'd just blurted out the offer without thinking about it. "It's a loft, actually. Over the Bluebird Bakery a couple of blocks down from the office."

"I didn't know there were lofts over the bakery."

"Just one loft. The other half of the top floor is storage for the bakery. I was in there a couple of years ago, getting a cake for—well, it doesn't really matter what it was for. I was getting a cake, and Mr. McMinn was complaining about all the empty space he had now that a lot of his goods are shipped in daily from the processing plant in Maryville, and I said something about how businesses in the big cities are selling or renting space above their stores as residential lofts, and then he said he didn't even know if his business could be zoned for residential use, so I went to city hall and asked." He stopped as if he'd run out of words. Or breath. Or both.

"And they said yes?"

He nodded. "I bought half the space, outright. And then I did the work myself, after hours and on weekends. It's still a little rough, but that's how lofts are supposed to be, if you ask me. Which you didn't."

He was nervous, she realized. About asking her to stay with him? "I don't want to put you out."

"You wouldn't be. There's a ton of space. And the bedroom is partitioned off from the rest of the loft, so you'd have privacy."

Oh. Privacy.

What had she been thinking, that he wanted her there for other reasons?

"What about you?" she asked. "Where will you sleep?"

"I don't sleep," he said with a grin.

She made herself smile back at him. "What, you're a vampire like Mr. Quinn?"

As soon as the words left her mouth, she saw Anson's gaze shift away from her to something behind her, his eyes widening. A second later, she realized why.

"The rumors of my immortality are greatly exaggerated," Alexander Quinn murmured from behind her.

She turned around to face her boss, mortified. "I am so sorry."

Quinn's expression was hard to read, as usual. "I see Mr. Daughtry has been spreading rumors again."

"I think it adds to your mystique," Anson said lightly, his earlier nervousness gone.

Maybe he was only nervous with her. But why? She was about the least intimidating person in the world.

"I shouldn't have said—" she began.

Quinn waved her off. "I don't mind my employees thinking I'm a supernatural being. I rather cultivate the notion." He focused his penetrating gaze on her, his hazel-green eyes uncharacteristically warm. "You seem to have had yourself an eventful night."

"I'm fine," she said quickly. "It's Anson you should worry about. He took a pretty bad beating earlier this evening, and now he's walking around pretending he's fine."

"I am fine," Anson said. "I mean, sure, my body feels like one big ache, but the doctors assured me none of my injuries are life-threatening."

"You both should get out of here. Get some sleep."

"I was just telling Anson I should probably get a hotel room here in town—"

"I don't think it's a good idea for her to be alone in a hotel room, considering the fact that she and her brother are clearly targets," Anson interrupted, slanting a look at her before lifting his gaze back to meet Quinn's again. "I suggested the loft."

One of Quinn's sandy-brown eyebrows notched upward, but he just looked at Ginny. "Would you be comfortable with that?"

She wasn't sure how to answer. Did Quinn actually think it was a good idea for her to stay with a man she barely knew in his loft apartment?

"I think she's not sure she can trust me as a bodyguard," Anson said in a quiet tone. She looked up quickly to see if he was making a joke, but he looked serious.

"I didn't say— That's not—" She sighed. "I have no complaints about your protective skills. Not after tonight."

"Then it's settled," Quinn said in a flat tone that suggested arguments would be futile. "Get her out of here, Daughtry. You both look like you're about to collapse." He turned and walked back down the corridor toward Danny's room.

"Does anyone ever tell him no?" she asked.

"On occasion. They don't live long enough to tell about it." Anson flattened his hand against her back, his touch warm and bracing. "If you want to say no, you should. I get that you don't really know me, and this has been a rough night for you—"

"I'm really tired. And I don't like the idea of staying alone, so—" She looked up at him, looking past his battered face to the melted-chocolate eyes. "I'd really like to go to the loft, if the offer still stands."

"I'D JUST LIKE to point out that I'm a bachelor and I wasn't expecting guests," Anson said as he unlocked the door to the converted storage space he'd turned into home sweet home. Fortunately, he'd had a lot of time on his hands over the past few weeks, giving him time to clean up after himself and do some of the chores he normally put off when he was working long hours at The Gates.

On the downside, he'd been putting his hand to some of the building projects he'd been meaning to get around to for months, which meant that one side of the loft's wide-open space was filled with sawhorses and tools.

"You weren't kidding about doing the work yourself," Ginny commented, taking in the half-finished built-in bookcase that would eventually fill the far wall.

"My dad was a carpenter," he said, trying to remember the good times, as rare as they'd been. His father's lessons in woodworking had usually included insults and the occasional slap or shove, but Anson had made himself learn the lessons anyway, trying to separate the knowledge from the mean drunk who'd imparted it.

"So he taught you to build cabinets?"

"Cabinets, chairs, tables. The usual."

"And you became a computer whiz instead."

He glanced at her, enjoying the quiet stillness

of her beauty. Clean-faced and sleepy-eyed, with her soft blond hair a tousled mess, she was still about the prettiest thing he'd ever seen in his life.

"What?" she asked, making him realize he'd been staring at her.

"Just not used to seeing a woman in this place," he blurted, then realized it made him sound like a complete loser.

"You don't bring women here?"

"No."

Her eyes narrowed slightly. "Men?"

He grinned. "No. Not them, either."

"Hmm." She looked at him for a moment, her head tilted as if she was looking for an answer to some question she hadn't asked aloud. Then she turned toward the large windows that took up the wall facing Magnolia Avenue, a faint smile touching her lips.

She crossed to the windows, drawn there by the loft's best feature—the view of the Smoky Mountains rising above the town to the east. The sun hadn't yet risen, but the first rosy light of the coming dawn flirted with the eastern sky, back-lighting the mist-shrouded mountains.

He moved to stand beside her. "And now you get why I decided living in a storage space above a bakery was a good idea."

"You're a lucky man to wake up to that view every morning."

"I know I'm lucky. Things for me could have turned out a lot worse."

She shot him a quizzical look, but she didn't ask him to elaborate. So he didn't.

"You should get to bed."

She looked around the loft. "What bed?"

He gave her a little nudge to turn her toward the partition he'd built to hide the bedroom from the rest of the loft. "Go around that wall you see right there, the one with the big purple painting on it. On the other side is the bedroom."

She gave him another one of her narrow-eyed looks he was starting to get accustomed to before she picked up her duffel bag and headed for the wall he'd pointed out. She disappeared around the wall for a moment, then backed out, her eyes wide. Suddenly she scuttled back to his side. "Anson?" She spoke in a whisper.

He felt the first flutter of alarm in his belly. "What?"

"There's a woman sleeping in your bed."

Chapter Six

"Good God, Anson, what happened to your face?"

The brunette sitting in the middle of the pillows on Anson's bed was wearing his favorite Atlanta Braves T-shirt, her curves doing things to the cotton fabric that were probably illegal in some countries, and if she were any other woman, and he were any other man, he might find his surprise bed visitor a fantasy come true.

"Long story, Nicki." He glanced at Ginny, who had ventured out from behind him to regard the woman in the bed. "Ginny, this is Nicolette Jamison. My long-lost cousin."

"I saw you a year ago, Anson. Don't be so

melodramatic." She turned to Ginny, flashing a smile that was pure Nicki—straight white teeth, matching dimples and flashing blue eyes. "So, you're the new girlfriend?"

"Nicki—"

"Nice to meet you," Ginny interrupted, slanting a look at Anson that made his stomach twist into knots. "I'm just a friend in need of a place to crash for a few hours. Anson offered his bed. He must have forgotten you were coming."

"Oh, he didn't know," Nicki said brightly with a wave of her hand. "I was sort of in the need of the same thing—a place to crash. Got here well after midnight and knocked until my knuckles were bruised, but no answer. So I figured he was probably out for the night."

"And so you took out your handy-dandy lock pick and let yourself in?" Anson picked up the jeans she'd dropped on the floor by his bed and tossed them at her.

Nicki caught them. "I made a copy of your key

the last time I was here. I figured it might come in handy someday."

He wanted to be angry at her, but trying to stay angry at Nicki was like trying to bail out the ocean with a teacup. "You'll be giving that back to me before you leave."

She frowned at him. "Fine way to treat family."

He knew she wasn't really hurt. She knew as well as he did that she'd crossed a line. Crossing lines was one of her favorite pastimes. "How long are you going to be in town this time?"

"I'm thinking of sticking around, actually," she answered, motioning for him to turn his back.

With a sigh, he turned around, folding his arms across his chest. Ginny turned toward him, her sandy eyebrows arching slightly.

"I'm sorry about this," he murmured.

She shook her head. "I have no room to talk about family issues."

"Y'all do know I'm sitting right here, don't you?" Nicki asked.

Anson heard a zipping noise and turned around

to look at her. She was still stretching out his Braves T-shirt in all the wrong places, but at least she was dressed and ready to get the hell out of his place. He could buy another shirt. "You got enough money to get you a hotel room somewhere?"

She grimaced. "You're really not going to let me stay?"

Anson sighed. "I have one bed. It's going to be occupied for the next few hours and not by you."

"Anson, it's okay, she can stay," Ginny said. "I'm the stranger. I'll find a room—"

"No, he's right," Nicki said quickly, flashing another one of her perfect smiles. "I can be a pain in the butt. Sometimes that works in my favor. Today it didn't." She slipped her feet into a pair of sneakers and looked up at Anson. "Can I keep the T-shirt?"

"Please," he said with a wave of his hand.

She grinned at him, and he forgot why he was angry. "I'll be around. I'll call you. Maybe you'll be in a better mood." She grabbed the enormous purse sitting on the bedside table and looked around the room until she spotted a faded army surplus backpack sitting against the wall next to the large wardrobe cabinet. She grabbed it and smiled at Ginny. "It really was nice to meet you. Anson's taste in 'friends' is improving."

As she started to sweep past him, Anson reached out and caught her arm. "The key?"

She sighed and handed him the backpack. It weighed a ton. Digging in her purse, she shot him a quick grin. "I never could sneak anything past you. Inconvenient, having a genius for a cousin."

"Sucking up isn't going to make me let you keep the key, Nick." But he softened his words with a smile.

She handed him the key and threw her arms around him, giving him a fierce hug. "Not sucking up. And I'm serious about sticking around this time." She let him go and looked up at him. "I'm feeling the need for roots."

He wasn't sure the rocky soil of Purgatory, Tennessee, was the place for a woman like Nicki to put down roots, but he wouldn't mind if she stayed awhile. She might be nothing but trouble, but she was the only family he had left. "Call me when you get settled somewhere."

"Will do." She waggled her fingers at Ginny and left the bedroom nook, moving at a breezy clip. A few seconds later, he heard the door close behind her.

"Hurricane Nicolette," he murmured.

"Why did you do that?" Ginny asked, her voice tight.

He looked up to find her frowning at him. "Do what? Kick Nicki out?"

"She's your family."

"She's a cousin I see every few years. She won't stick around this time, either. And she's trouble."

"She's still your family. Do you have any idea what it's like not to have any family? Danny's all I have in the world. Everybody else is either dead or gone. Maybe you have enough family to be able to turn your back on someone just because she annoys you, but—"

"She's the only family I have," he interrupted. "But unlike you, I don't let her walk all over me."

As soon as he said the words, he regretted them. But it was too late. Ginny's eyes widened as if he'd slapped her.

"I don't let him walk all over me. But he needs help. And unlike *you*, I'm not coldhearted enough to kick someone I love out of my life when it's inconvenient." She started past him, her jaw tightly set.

He caught her arm, and she snapped her angry gaze up to meet his.

"You know you can't walk out of here like this."

She jerked her arm away. "I can. The office is two blocks down and I have a key to the place. I'll crash on the sofa in the break room." She strode away from him.

"I'm sorry," he said, following her back to the main room of the loft. "I was irritated by Nicki and I said something stupid."

She whipped around to face him. "Something

stupid that you meant. You're not apologizing for thinking it. Just for saying it. Right?"

He took a deep breath through his nose. "If he's selling drugs out of your house, you could be sucked into his trouble, too. You know that, right?"

"Of course I know that." Her strangled tone revealed a hint of the turmoil he saw roiling behind her eyes. "Someone stabbed him and broke into my house. You had to flush drugs down my toilet and hide the evidence to protect us. If you think I'm unaware of those facts, then you must think I'm a complete imbecile."

"I think you're a kind, compassionate woman who loves her brother and wants desperately to protect him." The urge to touch her face, to smooth the worry lines away from her brow, caught him flat-footed. He clenched his fists by his sides. "I know you don't want to turn your back on him or cause him any pain, but he's not giving you the same consideration, is he?"

She bit her lower lip but didn't reply.

He took a step closer. "I'm not trying to hurt you. I don't mean to dismiss your feelings. I'm not very good at communicating, I guess."

Her expression softened as she met his gaze again. "You think?"

He smiled. "Stay. I just cleared out the bed for you."

"And ran off your poor cousin."

He almost laughed at the thought. "Nicki would probably flatten you if she heard you call her my poor cousin. She's tough. She's smarter than either one of us, and she always, always lands on her feet."

"I just hate that she has to do that because of me."

A lock of hair had fallen across her cheek. He couldn't stop himself from brushing it back from her pale face. "I would have kicked her out anyway for stealing a copy of my key and presuming that she can invade my privacy anytime she wants to."

Ginny gave him an odd look, and he dropped his hand back to his side.

"Sorry," he murmured.

"Are you sure she's going to be okay out there?"

"It's Purgatory. She'll run down to the diner on Main and before you know it, some poor farmer's family will have taken her in and given her a room of her own. Trust me. She'll be fine." He waved his arm toward the bedroom. "We've just wasted thirty minutes of prime sleeping time on my cousin. Go get some rest. You're going to need your strength when we get back to the hospital."

She glanced toward the wall that shielded the bedroom from the rest of the loft. He could see the warring emotions behind her soft blue eyes—the need for sleep battling with the need to not depend on anyone else. Weariness won, and she picked up her duffel bag and carried it with her as she went back into the bedroom.

Anson dropped onto the sofa and kicked off his shoes, sinking into the soft cushions. Every inch of his body ached, and he wished he could take a shower, but the shower was hidden behind the bedroom wall with Ginny.

He twisted himself around until his head was on the arm of the sofa and his feet hung off the other end. Not the most comfortable of positions, and if he thought his body was hurting now, he could only imagine how bad it would be when he woke up again. But he was too tired to move again.

Unfortunately, his phone vibrated against his butt, proving him wrong. He *could* move again, at least enough to shift his body to get the phone out of his back pocket.

He checked the display. Quinn. Of course.

"Sorry, you have reached the phone of Anson Daughtry. He just got the hell kicked out of him, was chased by gun-toting drug thugs and spent all night dealing with the aftermath. Leave a message and he'll get back to you—if he lives through the morning."

"Why did your cousin just walk through the

door of my agency and ask for a job, giving you as a reference?"

Anson groaned. "Were you kind when you kicked her out? Wait, stupid question. You're never kind."

"Actually, I'm thinking about hiring her."

He sat up quickly, biting back a groan as the quick movement sent shivers of pain racing up and down his bruised ribs. "That's a joke, right?"

"We need someone to infiltrate the BRI. She's from this area, knows a lot of the players and nobody has any reason to suspect she'd be working for an investigative agency."

That was true, Anson had to concede. "She has no undercover experience."

"Actually, according to her, she does. She said she was a confidential informant for the Nashville Police Department for over a year."

Anson rubbed his face. "I'd check her references carefully. Nicki and the truth have always been little more than acquaintances."

"I did check. She's legit. And, according to the

detective I talked to, she was invaluable in helping the NPD bring down a ring of auto thieves."

"Probably because she was dating one of the carjackers."

"I'm going to have McGee in Human Resources give her a more thorough vetting, but if she checks out, I'm using her."

"Was this your idea or hers?"

"Hers."

"She offered herself as an undercover operative?"

"I take it she didn't tell you why she was back in Purgatory?"

Anson closed his eyes, leaning back against the sofa cushions. "I didn't give her much of a chance," he admitted.

"I'm sure she'll be in touch. Next time, shut up and listen." Quinn hung up the phone.

With a grimace, Anson leaned forward and put his phone on the coffee table, a twisting sensation in his gut. He wished he could blame it on hunger, but he'd be lying to himself.

He was worried. About Nicki. About Ginny Coltrane and her troubled brother.

And, if he was being truthful, about himself, as well. He wasn't a trained agent like Brand or the other men and women who'd come to his rescue tonight. He certainly wasn't tough enough to keep four big, burly thugs from kicking him to a pulp.

What the hell made him think he could protect anyone from the trouble headed their way?

GINNY HADN'T THOUGHT she could sleep in the strange bed, with anxiety flopping around in her gut like a fish out of water, but the quality of light that greeted her the next time she opened her eyes proved she'd been wrong. She rubbed the sleep from her eyes and checked her watch. Nearly two in the afternoon. She'd slept for almost eight hours.

She also really had to use the bathroom—and had no idea where it was.

There was a door on one side of the bedroom

area that looked promising. She shoved off the covers and padded barefoot across the room to open the door. Inside, she found sheer heaven.

The bathroom was spacious, with tall ceilings and a large picture window looking out across the rolling farmlands that stretched west of Purgatory for several miles. The day was clear and sunny, drenching the scene with color and life, and she almost forgot why she'd been looking for the bathroom in the first place.

When she was done, she explored the bathroom a little more thoroughly, taking in the enormous old claw-foot tub and the detached shower that was roomy and inviting. The thought of a shower was more than she could resist, and she had already shucked off her shirt when a soft knock on the door stopped her cold.

"Ginny?" Anson sounded reluctant to interrupt.

With a sigh, she pulled her shirt back on and opened the bathroom door. Anson stood on the other side, looking rumpled and apologetic.

"I just got a call from the hospital. Danny's awake. And he won't talk to anyone but you."

ANSON HAD CONVINCED Ginny she could stop long enough to take a shower, change clothes and wait while he did the same. Though his aching bones argued for a long, hot soak, he made it quick, and they were back at the hospital in Knoxville within an hour.

Caleb Cooper stood outside Danny's hospital room door in a loose-limbed slouch belied by his sharp green eyes. He straightened at the sight of Ginny, flashing her a wide smile. "Hey there, Ginny."

She smiled back. "Hi, Caleb."

No "Mr. Cooper" for the new guy, Anson thought with a frown.

"He's doing a lot better than last night, physically," Caleb told them cheerily. "The doctor told him everything is looking really good, better than they could have expected, given the state his liver's probably in."

Ginny frowned. "Could you say that a little louder? I don't think the rest of the hospital heard you."

"Sorry." Caleb looked duly chastised, his ruddy face flushing. Anson bit back a grin.

"You tried questioning him about the drugs?" Ginny asked.

Caleb nodded. "The lab test came back shortly before lunch. High-grade cocaine. Barely cut with anything yet. If they're planning to market the stuff in this neck of the woods, they're going to have to make it a lot more affordable."

"Or they're acting as a distributor, shipping out the good stuff to better-paying customers in the cities," Anson suggested.

Caleb considered the idea. "Maybe. But if it's the BRI, they may be setting up a wholesale operation instead. Selling the good stuff to the smaller dealers to cut themselves. Gives them a lot more power that way—the little guys come to depend on them for the supply."

Anson hadn't thought of that possibility, but it

made sense, especially if Quinn was right about the BRI going into the drug trade themselves in a more direct way. "You think the BRI has better connections to the South American suppliers than the individual dealers?"

Caleb nodded. "That's our theory."

And Quinn was thinking about sending his cousin, Nicki, into that nest of vipers. Anson's gut knotted at the thought. "Has Quinn been here yet?"

"He left not long after you did. Headed to the office, I think." One corner of Caleb's mouth crooked. "He never sleeps, does he?"

"Seems that way," Anson conceded.

"Is Danny still awake?" Ginny looked up at Caleb with anxiety in her soft blue eyes.

"Yes. He's waiting for you."

Ginny shifted her gaze to Anson. He smiled encouragingly, and she lifted her chin and opened the hospital room door.

Once she'd closed the door behind her, Anson turned to Caleb. "He didn't say anything to you?"

"Not yet. I'm hoping Ginny can make him see that cooperating with us is his safest course of action. Assuming he's an innocent pawn in the BRI's game, that is."

Anson arched an eyebrow. "You think he's not?"

"I think that was a hell of a lot of coke to entrust to a drunk unless he's up to his eyeballs in the operation. Do you think the BRI would take that risk just to use him as a mule?"

"I don't know," Anson admitted. What he knew about the drug trade could fit on the back of a postcard. His drug of choice was caffeine. "Ginny seems so certain her brother is being duped."

Caleb shrugged, settling back into his lazy slouch. "Maybe he is."

But maybe he's not, Anson thought, wishing he was on the other side of that hospital room door.

"I DON'T KNOW why they're keeping me in here. I'm fine." Danny grimaced at Ginny, looking like a petulant teenager.

She sighed. "You were stabbed. You have a liver laceration. You're at risk of infection."

"They're trying to dry me out like some sort of sloppy drunk. I just like to drink sometimes. What's the big deal?"

"Did you hear me mention a liver laceration? You don't need to put any alcohol through your liver while the wound is healing."

He pressed his lips into a thin line of irritation. "Fine. I'll stay here and play the perfect patient."

He hadn't asked anything about the stabbing, Ginny thought. Had it not occurred to him to ask? Or did he already know who'd attacked him?

She decided to go with a direct approach. "Did you see those men last night at the bar? In the parking lot?"

He frowned. "I don't really remember that much about last night. I think you were there, weren't you, Gigi?"

She hated when he used his childhood nickname for her. He only did it when he was drunk—or trying to manipulate her emotions.

"I was there. I could have been seriously hurt by those guys."

He reached out and took the hand she'd laid on the bed beside him. "I would have been gutted if you'd gotten hurt. You know that, don't you?"

Maybe he would have been, once he sobered up. "Do you know why those men were after you?"

He shook his head. "Not a clue. Maybe they're just into robbing guys who've had a little too much to drink."

"Do they normally show up outside your hospital room to finish the job? Or break into your house in case they missed something the first time they tried to rob you?"

Danny's brow creased. "You're saying that happened?"

"You had a big baggie full of coke stashed in your drawer."

The frown turned to a scowl. "You went through my stuff? God, Ginny!"

"I was trying to get you a change of clothes so

you'd be more comfortable." She waved at the cabinet near the bed. "There are a few things in there for you."

"You sure you didn't just use that as an excuse to check up on me?"

"Don't change the subject. Are you using?"

"No."

"Then why were you hiding a bag of coke in your drawer?"

Danny's expression went stony. "What bag of coke?"

"You're trying to pretend it wasn't in your drawer the last time you checked?"

"I have no idea what you're talking about," Danny answered. And to her surprise, he sounded completely earnest.

Was it possible someone had planted the drugs in his room?

A new, darker thought occurred to her—could Anson have planted the coke in Danny's drawer?

He was on administrative leave at The Gates, after all. Quinn clearly still saw him as a suspect in the leaks going on at the agency. Leaks that had put the life of another computer expert in grave danger from dangerous Colombian gunrunners.

How likely was it that gunrunners from Colombia weren't also involved with the drug trade?

"What are you thinking?" Danny asked.

She looked at him. "I think you need to rest. And then, when you're feeling better, you need to tell Caleb Cooper anything and everything you know about the men who attacked you."

"I said I don't know them—"

"They seem to know you. So you need to think long and hard about what you've been doing over the last few months and why something like that might tick off a bunch of self-styled militia thugs." She rose from the chair next to his bed. "I'll be back later."

"Where are you going?" Danny asked.

"I need to talk to someone." She laid her hand on his arm, giving it a light squeeze. "Try to sleep, okay? It's the best thing you can do for your healing process."

She stepped outside the room. Caleb was still there, but Anson was nowhere around.

Good.

She pulled out her phone and dialed a number she'd stored the night before. Alexander Quinn answered on the second ring. "Marbury Motors—"

"We need to talk," she said.

Chapter Seven

"She's not in there," Caleb told Anson when he returned from a trip to the cafeteria.

"Where is she?" He'd picked up a couple of cans of soda and a small selection of sandwiches for her to choose from. She had to be starving by now, since they hadn't stopped to eat anything before heading to the hospital that afternoon.

"I don't know. She came out, made a call and next thing I know, she told me she'd be back in a little while."

Anson frowned. "You let her go?"

"I'm not a jailer."

"Someone broke into her house last night. Someone stabbed her brother and threatened her.

And you just let her walk away unescorted?" Anson glared at Caleb.

Caleb rose to his full height—only an inch shorter than Anson—and flexed his broad shoulders in a clear display of testosterone. "She's a grown woman capable of making her own decisions. Besides, she came with you, right? Her car is in the shop. Where's she going to go?"

Caleb had a point. Without wheels, she couldn't get that far. Maybe she'd gone down to the gift shop.

But whom had she called?

"If she comes back, tell her to stay put until I can catch up with her. And watch this." He put the bag of food and drinks on the floor next to Caleb and headed for the elevators, pulling out his phone to hunt for her phone number in his call log. Locating it, he hit the "redial" button.

The call went straight to voice mail. He almost hung up, then thought better of it and left a message. "Ginny, it's Anson. I'm looking for you. Call me back."

On the lobby floor, he found the gift shop and looked around for Ginny, but she wasn't there. She wasn't in the lobby, either. And he hadn't seen her in the rest area at the end of the seventh floor corridor, either.

Where the hell had she gone?

"I DON'T LIKE to be summoned." Quinn greeted her in a flat tone, waving toward the bench outside the hospital entrance.

Ginny sat down, leaving him room to join her. "I needed to know something about your investigation into the information leaks at The Gates."

"It's an ongoing investigation."

"Anson Daughtry is your only suspect."

"He's the only one we've identified."

"You think he's working in collusion with someone else?"

Quinn's expression didn't change, but the look in his eyes became more shuttered. "You're assuming I think he's the mole."

"He's on administrative leave."

"As was Nick Darcy. Until he proved to me that he wasn't involved in the leaks."

"And Daughtry hasn't proved his innocence."

"Is there a point to these questions?"

Ginny licked her lips, feeling both scared and ungrateful. Until her brother had suggested the drugs might be part of a frame-up, she hadn't even considered the idea that Anson might be snowing her. But there had to be a reason he was a suspect in the information leaks. "I need to know more about what you suspect Daughtry might be involved in. All I know is that it's about information leaks. And it has something to do with an attack on Mara Jennings. She was hired as a runner, but you had her doing something else, didn't you?"

She could tell from the flicker of irritation in Quinn's eyes that she knew more than he had realized. "What makes you think that?"

"I do most of the billing paperwork at the agency. I know what you paid her and what runners are normally paid." She realized, with some trepidation, that what she was about to reveal might make her a suspect in the leak case, as well. But Danny's life was on the line. She had to take a risk. "She was targeted by Colombian gunrunners, wasn't she?"

Quinn didn't answer. He didn't have to. The sheer stillness of his expression and the opacity of his stony gaze told her she was on the right track. She was finally beginning to be able to read her inscrutable boss.

"She disappeared shortly after an article appeared in the paper about gunrunners from Medellín getting killed in a confrontation with an unnamed police agency. But it wasn't the police, was it? It was agents from The Gates." She didn't expect him to respond, so she continued, "Her sister was murdered in Amarillo a few years ago. I did some checking into her background when she left the agency without giving notice."

"Why would that even occur to you? You're an administrative assistant, not an agent."

She met his gaze without flinching, tired of

everyone treating her like a hothouse flower. "I have a brain. One that doesn't get used a lot in my job. And I'm curious by nature."

"You realize you've just made yourself a suspect in the leak investigation."

"Yes, I do. But I need to know if you believe Anson Daughtry has it in him to plant cocaine in my brother's dresser drawer. I need to know why he's been so Johnny-on-the-spot since this whole mess started. Why was he at the bar last night to begin with?"

"I imagine to get a drink."

"I made a call to the Whiskey Road Tavern while I was waiting for you to arrive. I talked to the bartender, Jase. He and Anson are friends. I pretended I'd just called to thank him, but I asked a few questions about Anson while I was at it. Pretended I was potentially interested in Anson romantically—"

"Are you?" Quinn asked.

"I asked Jase if Anson was a big drinker. I hinted that I was wary of getting involved with someone who couldn't control himself around booze. Easy to sell it, given my problems with Danny and his drinking."

"And what did you learn?" Quinn was careful to mask his thoughts.

"Anson doesn't drink at all. His father was an alcoholic. As a result, Anson's a teetotaler."

"People go to bars for other things besides liquor."

"They do," she conceded. "But Anson doesn't. Jase said it was the first time he'd seen him anywhere near the bar in years. They usually meet somewhere else because Anson doesn't even like the smell of liquor."

"So why do you think he was there?" Quinn asked.

"I don't know." She looked down at her hands, saw that she'd clenched them together so tightly that her knuckles had turned white. She made herself relax, loosened the death grip of her fingers on each other. "I don't want to believe he had an ulterior motive for being there. But he was so on the spot. I mean, he waded right into the mess, one of him against four of them—why would he have done that for someone he barely knew by sight?"

"Some people are just that way."

"Your agents, maybe. I mean, half of them are war heroes or former feds who are used to putting their lives on the line. But Anson Daughtry is a computer genius. His life is computers, not weapons and hand-to-hand combat. Why didn't he just call the police when he saw trouble brewing?"

"Because they were at least ten minutes away." Anson's voice was a low growl over her left shoulder. "You could have been dead by then."

She whirled around to look up at him. He loomed behind her, a lanky giant wearing a hard scowl. "You were following me last night, weren't you?" she asked.

His lips pressed together but he didn't answer.

Quinn stood up. "I think the two of you need to talk. I'll go talk to Cooper and check on your brother." He nodded to Anson and headed for the hospital entrance.

Ginny looked down at her hands, feeling sick.

Anson walked past her and took Quinn's place on the bench, leaning forward with his arms on his knees. He didn't look at her, his gaze directed toward the sidewalk at his feet.

"Why were you asking Quinn all those questions about me?" he asked quietly.

"Why were you at the tavern last night?" she countered.

"Does it matter?"

She hated the evasive tone of his reply. "It does."

"I was following you."

She looked at him until he slowly turned to meet her gaze. His dark eyes were a whirlwind of guilt and anger.

The sick feeling only increased. "Why?"

He answered her question with one of his own. "How did you know I wasn't just there to get a drink?"

"You don't drink," she answered. "I called Jase at the tavern. Pretended I was interested in you. Romantically, I mean."

His nostrils flared and he looked away. "And somehow, the question of my alcohol aversion came up?"

"You don't even go to bars. So I had to wonder why you were there last night in the first place."

"Why did you call Jase? I mean, you said you were pretending to be interested in me to get information out of him, so you must have had your suspicions before you talked to him."

She licked her lips, not wanting to tell him what Danny had said.

"I left you with your brother, went down to the cafeteria to get us something to eat, and when I came back, you were gone. Caleb said you came out talking on your phone. To Quinn, I presume?"

"Yes."

He nodded slowly, giving her a sidelong glance. She thought she heard a hint of grudging admiration in his voice when he asked, "What did you do, summon him here to talk to you?"

"I couldn't go to him."

"Right. No wheels."

"I needed to know why you were a suspect in the leak investigation. I needed to know Quinn's opinion about your trustworthiness."

"What did he say?"

She released a huff of frustrated laughter. "You know Quinn. He never says anything that could come back to haunt him."

"Okay. So answer this—what made you suspicious of me in the first place? Was it the way I put my body in the way of four big, mean thugs to save you and your brother? Or was it the way I risked my life trying to evade gun-toting thugs who broke into your house while I was giving up sleep to get some clothes for the two of you? Or maybe it was the way I took you home and kicked out my cousin so you could get some much-needed sleep?"

"That's not fair," she growled.

"What did Danny tell you?" he asked quietly. "I presume that's what made you suspicious. Because you seemed to trust me before you walked in that room and talked to him."

She licked her lips, feeling ungrateful and furious at him for making her feel that way about suspicions that he himself admitted had some merit. "Does it matter why I was suspicious? You just admitted you were following me. But you didn't tell me why."

"What did Danny tell you?" he asked again.

"He said the drugs weren't his," she answered bluntly, her gaze snapping up to clash with his.

Anson stared at her, disbelieving. "And you think what? That I planted them in your house?"

"Why were you following me last night?" she asked.

"You believe your alcoholic brother when he says a bag of coke I found hidden in his dresser drawer isn't his? Your brother, the guy so drunk he couldn't walk himself out to your car last night?"

"He's never done drugs."

"That you know about."

"You followed me to the tavern last night!" Her voice rose as her control snapped. "You stalked me there. For all I know, you planned that whole encounter with those men—"

"And let them beat the hell out of me as a cover story?"

"I don't know!" All the tension of the past twenty-four hours seemed to crash down on her at once. She pressed her face into her hands, fighting tears with every ounce of strength left inside her.

She felt his hand slide between her shoulder blades, warm and comforting. She shrugged his touch away, not wanting to be vulnerable to him. Not now, when she didn't know who to believe.

He dropped his hand into his lap. When he spoke, he sounded weary and sad. "I was following you because I thought you might be the mole at The Gates."

"HAVE YOU TRIED talking to him again?" Quinn asked Caleb Cooper, knowing better than to fall for the agent's slacker persona. People who made the mistake of taking Caleb's laid-back appearance and casual style at face value were fools. And Quinn was no fool.

"I checked in after Daughtry came by with the food. Coltrane was asleep. Or feigning it. I don't think a blitz attack interrogation while he's in a hospital bed is going to be very effective with him."

"What do you think? Is he a dupe? Or is he in on it?"

"He's got all the classic traits of a dupe," Caleb said slowly.

"But?"

"One of the most effective disguises in the world is the harmless fool." Caleb's Southern drawl took on a hard edge. "If he's really faking it, he'll be hard to break. Especially with his sister guarding him like a mama bear."

Quinn frowned, remembering his earlier conversation with Ginny Coltrane. He'd had her figured for a smart woman or he'd have never hired her. He'd even thought, with time, she might fit very well into the fraud investigation section of the agency, with her attention to detail and her facility with numbers.

But the way she'd figured out several hidden details about the woman she knew as Mara Jennings showed a quickness of mind he hadn't anticipated. And the devious way she'd gone about investigating Anson Daughtry's story had taken him aback, and he wasn't a man who was easily surprised. He'd underestimated her skill set and thus her value to the agency. She might turn out to be one of his more inspired hires.

But like any human being, she had soft spots that could be exploited. Her brother was the most obvious pressure point, but she might have others.

In fact, she might be sitting next to one of them right this moment.

GINNY STARED AT him as if he'd spoken to her in Russian. Except maybe she spoke Russian, for all he knew. Or Swahili or Hindi or Dari or—

"Why would you think I was the mole at the agency?" She sounded completely poleaxed by his confession. "I'm not even an agent."

"Neither am I," he reminded her.

"But Quinn clearly has a reason to suspect you."

"And I had a reason to suspect you," he answered.

"Such as?"

"I knew I wasn't the mole. And Quinn clearly believes Nick Darcy isn't. And we, along with Quinn, were the only people who knew the evidence that got leaked to the bad guys."

A shadow passed across her face, and he felt his gut tumble in response.

"Well, then, I could see you being suspicious of Darcy, but—" Her voice failed her. She cleared her throat.

"I didn't ever think it was Darcy. And since I knew I didn't do it, I decided to approach the question from a new direction. Clearly, only

Darcy and I knew the full truth about Mara Jennings, because we're the only people Quinn told."

"The full truth?"

"What she was doing for us."

Ginny's eyes narrowed, but she waited for him to continue.

"I wondered if there was anything about Mara's employment that would have sent up red flags for someone who wasn't an agent. And then I realized that anyone who handled the payroll could potentially figure it out."

"Which led you to me." Her expression shifted. "But why not the accountant?"

"Because you're the one who actually works at the agency and knows the job descriptions. You're the one who sends the payroll list to the accountant to issue paychecks. All he has is a list of names and amounts. He doesn't know how they earned the money or whether or not the pay is commensurate with the jobs they're doing."

"But I do." Ginny nodded slowly. "And you were right, in one way. I did suspect Mara Jennings was doing more for the company than just running errands. But I certainly didn't share those suspicions with anyone."

"I don't think you did." He sighed. "But apparently you think I'm some sort of drug-planting lunatic—"

"My brother swears he didn't know anything about the drugs." She looked up at him, her eyes damp with unspilled tears. "I barely know you."

"Look, I get it. I do. But I'm telling you, the drugs were there when I opened your brother's drawer. I flushed them down the toilet. I didn't call the cops. All to protect him—and you." He felt frustration burning in the center of his chest. "Do you know how damn tired I am of having to defend myself against accusations of things I didn't do? Things I would never, ever do? Do you know how it feels?"

The tears brimming in her eyes spilled. "Now I do. Because that's what you suspected of me, isn't it?"

"I didn't want to." The urge to wipe those tears

from her cheeks was almost more than he could bear. He clenched his hands together between his knees and looked down at his feet. "I didn't want to think it was you, Ginny. I just didn't know where else to look."

"I guess I can understand that." She sniffed, lifting her hands to her face. When he looked at her again, she'd wiped the tear tracks from her cheeks. "I didn't want to think you could plant drugs in my house, either. But the alternative..."

"Is having to believe your brother might be dealing drugs," he finished for her. "I know. I don't want you to have to believe that, either."

"But if you didn't do it, who would have?" She sounded so defeated, so stripped of hope it made his chest ache.

"I don't know. I can't think of any good reason to frame him, can you?"

"I still don't know why those men were after him at the tavern last night," she murmured. "Or why one of them risked coming after him right here in the hospital."

"Or why they broke into your house while I was there," he added. "All important questions, I think."

She sighed. "If Danny knows the truth, he's not telling. And if he's lying, he's gotten so good at it that I can't tell anymore."

He knew she didn't want to believe her brother was lying to her. But he had the good sense not to say so aloud. Instead, he said, "I picked up some food if you're hungry. I left it with Caleb outside your brother's room."

"I'm not really hungry." She shook her head.

"Think of it as fuel. If you don't eat, you'll run out of energy, probably when you need it the most." He stood up and held out his hand to her.

She looked at his outstretched hand for a long moment. Then she placed her hand in his and stood, as well. He let his touch linger a second or two longer than he should have before he let go and nodded toward the hospital entrance.

In the elevator, somewhere between the third

and fourth floors, Anson's cell phone rang. It was Quinn. "Hey, boss."

"Is Ginny Coltrane still with you?" The tension in Quinn's voice set Anson's own nerves humming.

"Yes," he answered carefully.

"She needs to get up here now."

"What's going on?"

"Her brother's removed all his monitoring equipment, ripped out his IV and is demanding to leave."

Chapter Eight

The sight of Danny pinned between Caleb Cooper and a burly male nurse made Ginny's heart ache. He looked pale and sweaty, his blood dripping on the floor from the place in his hand where he'd removed the IV cannula.

"Danny, stop it!" She moved past Quinn and stopped in front of her wild-eyed brother, catching his chin in her hand.

He jerked his face away, but at least her touch had gotten his attention. His eyes focused on hers, settled there and softened at the sight of her. "Gigi."

"What's the matter, Danny? We talked about

how important it was for you to stay here and get well. You said you understood, remember?"

"They're killing me in here," he said in a plaintive tone.

"No, they're not," she said firmly, grabbing a tissue from the box on the bedside table. "Let's stop that bleeding."

He let her take his hand, wincing as she applied pressure to stop the bleeding from the open vein. She glanced at the nurse, who gave a nod and released Danny's right arm. But Caleb kept his hands firmly around Danny's left arm, his expression watchful and stern.

Nodding at Caleb to help her, she led Danny back to the bed. "Sit down. Let's see if the doctor will let you lose the IV. How about that?"

"I'll get the doctor," the nurse said, heading for the door.

"What made you think you needed to leave?" she asked Danny in a quiet voice, glancing over her shoulder to see where Anson was. He stood next to Quinn in the doorway, watching her, his dark eyes narrowed and his expression unreadable.

"I just want to go home. I want my own bed and my own food."

"And your stash of liquor in your sock drawer?" she asked.

His gaze snapped up to meet hers. "You snooping bitch!"

The snarling rage shocked her so much she flinched. Danny had never spoken to her that way before.

Never.

"Enough," Anson said, stepping into the room. He put his hand on Ginny's shoulder, gently tugging her away from the bed. She let him, her knees shaking too hard for her to do anything but drop into the nearby chair.

Anson stepped between her and Danny, towering over the bed. "Ginny didn't find the liquor. I did. I was looking for clothes for you."

"Who the hell are you?" Danny growled.

"I'm the man who took a beating last night

so your sister could get help and save your un-grateful ass," Anson replied, sounding utterly unmoved by Danny's hostility. In fact, Ginny heard a note of fury that caught her by surprise. "And I don't personally give a damn if you drink yourself to death. You wouldn't be the first and you sure as hell won't be the last. But your sister cares, and I don't think she deserves your wrath, do you? After everything she's done for you, tak-ing you in and making sure you have a home and food to eat and clothes to wear—"

"You're right," Danny said, tears in his voice. "I'm so sorry, Gigi."

God help her, she wanted to believe him.

"Don't buy it, Ginny." Anson turned to look at her, his expression hard. He looked different, she thought, a chill running up her spine. Dangerous.

"Maybe we should all clear out and give the nurse time to make sure Danny didn't pull out any stitches?" Quinn suggested in a tone so calm and reasonable it made Ginny feel like a hysteric.

"Good idea," Anson growled, stalking out of the room in four swift strides.

"Gigi?" Danny's plaintive voice drew her attention back to him. She crossed to his bedside but didn't take the hand he stretched out to her.

"Do what the nurse tells you to do. Don't give him any more trouble. Do you understand me?"

Danny's eyes narrowed at her cool tone. "Yeah, I get it. Your new boyfriend snaps his fingers, you come to heel. Is that it?"

She turned to walk away, both hurt and furious. Danny caught her wrist, holding her in place.

"I'm sorry," he said again, his tone sincere. "I don't know why I'm being such a bastard to you—"

"Because you want a drink and you can't have one. And that pisses you off and you take it out on me because you know I'll let you." She pulled her wrist away from his grasp. "That changes now. Are we clear?"

He nodded.

"I'll be back to check on you in a little while."

She turned and left, hiding her tears until she was out the door.

Quinn was waiting for her. "You handled that very well."

She wiped the tears from her eyes with her fingertips, angry that she'd let them fall at all. "Not nearly soon enough."

"Family is…complicated."

She eyed him, wondering if he even had a family. Quinn was one of those people who seemed to have sprung, fully grown, into the world. She couldn't picture him as a child, couldn't see him playing with a teddy bear or Hot Wheels. G.I. Joe, maybe, she thought with a touch of amusement. He'd probably send ole Joe on some super-secret assignment to whatever war-torn country needed its pot stirred—

She saw an answering hint of amusement in Quinn's eyes, as if he could read her thoughts. She caught herself up quickly and looked around for Anson.

"Down the hall," Quinn said.

So he can read minds, too, she thought as she followed his gaze. Or, at least, situations.

Anson was sitting at the far end of the hospital corridor, where the hospital had set up a sofa and a couple of chairs for the comfort of visitors who didn't want to stay in the waiting room located on the floor below. He sat with his head back against the sofa and his gaze directed upward, his long legs stretched out in front of him.

She walked slowly down the hall to him, feeling an odd little thrill dance through her when he turned his head and settled his dark gaze on her. "I'm not going to apologize," he said.

"I didn't ask you to." She sat on one of the bowl-shaped chairs across from him, grimacing at the uncomfortable shape.

He edged down the sofa and patted the cushion next to him. "Whoever designed those chairs is probably in league with the devil."

She switched to the sofa, ignoring the urge to snuggle closer to Anson. "I told Danny things have to change."

He nodded. "Do you think he listened?"

"I'm not sure.

Anson sighed. "Until he's ready to admit he's got a problem he can't solve alone, you're going to see more and more of that kind of behavior from him. If you're smart, and I think you are, you won't let him twist you up about it, because he's going to try."

"I'm starting to get that."

"Don't let him wreck you, Ginny. There may come a point when you just need to let go."

"Like they say in Alcoholics Anonymous?" She turned to look at him. He sat with his profile to her, his gaze centered on the view outside the window at the end of the corridor. She followed his gaze and saw the hospital was positioned perfectly for a spectacular view of the Knoxville skyline, the round gold ball of the Sunsphere, a remnant of the 1982 World's Fair, glittering in the bright midday sunlight. "'Let go and let God'?"

"Let go." He turned to look at her, drawing her gaze back to him. "Or he'll destroy you."

"We're not talking about Danny anymore, are we?"

His gaze dropped to his long-fingered hands, clasped so tightly together his knuckles were white. "What do you want to do now? Go back to Danny?"

She shook her head. "He needs to decompress. Didn't you say something about food earlier?"

"Right." He stood with a slight grimace, as if the effort of unfolding his lanky body was uncomfortable. She imagined it probably was, if the rest of his body was as battered as his face. "I left the bag of food with Cooper. Not sure if he still has it."

She followed him down the hall to Danny's room. The door was closed, she saw. Quinn and Caleb stood outside, their heads close in conversation.

Quinn looked up at their approach. "The nurse settled him down. Gave him something to sleep."

"Did anyone check out that nurse?" Anson asked. "Remember, that guy I chased right here in the hospital was dressed as an orderly."

"Yes," Quinn answered bluntly. "The hospital administrator supplied us with a list of personnel who work this floor, complete with photo ID. We're monitoring all comings and goings."

Ginny shook her head, wondering at how easily Quinn seemed to accomplish tasks that most people would have to jump through hoops to get done. The joke around the office was that Quinn's time in the CIA meant he had top secret dossiers on everyone and wasn't afraid to use them to get his way. Sometimes, Ginny almost believed the joke was true.

"What did you do with the food?" Anson asked Caleb.

"Sorry, man. It sort of got stomped all over during the melee." Caleb grimaced. "Had to throw it away."

Quinn reached into his pocket, pulled out a thin silver money clip and peeled off a couple of twenties. "Why don't you two get out of here for a little while? There are a couple of nice restaurants in walking distance."

Anson looked at Ginny, a question mark in his expression.

"Good idea," she murmured in response.

He nodded toward the elevators, waiting for her to move before he followed. She felt his hand brush the small of her back as he ushered her into the next available elevator car.

"You don't have to eat with me if you'd rather I just go the hell away," he said quietly once the doors shut behind them.

"I could use the company." Looking up, she found him gazing at her, his expression vulnerable. She ventured a smile and the look of relief that swept across his face made her want to cry.

"I know I pissed you off, the way I treated your brother," he said a moment later. "I'm sorry about that. I mean, the part where I made you angry."

"But not for what you said to him?"

He sighed. "No. Not sorry about that."

The elevator dinged as they reached the lobby level, and the doors glided open. Once again, Anson's fingertips played against her back, and she couldn't quite suppress a shiver of pure animal awareness at his touch.

He was nothing like any man she'd ever known. Nothing like the kind of men she normally found attractive.

And yet, there was something so solid, so quixotically heroic about him that she found herself feeling like a giddy teenager in the throes of her first big crush whenever his melted-chocolate eyes focused on her, as they were at that very moment.

"What kind of food are you in the mood for?" he asked.

"I don't think I care," she admitted. "Right now, I just need fuel."

His gaze detached from hers to look up the street. The two restaurants Quinn had referred to sat on opposite sides of the street, across from one another. One was a deli, the other a Japanese sushi restaurant. "How adventurous are you, then?" he asked.

She'd never had sushi in her life. But she had a sudden urge to do something different, for once. Take a step outside the lines of her carefully drawn life and try something new.

"Very," she answered.

And hoped she wasn't making a big mistake.

THE LOOK ON Ginny's face when she saw the spider roll he'd ordered for her was priceless. She looked up at him, her blue eyes wide, as if she wanted to ask him if the crispy fried legs sticking out of either end of the roll belonged to an actual spider.

"Soft-shell crab," he answered her unasked question. "I guess I should have asked if you're allergic to shellfish."

"I'm not," she said, poking at the crab legs with one of the complimentary chopsticks, as if she expected them to poke back. "This isn't raw."

"I thought we'd ease you into the full sushi and

sashimi experience," he said. "Want some of the wasabi?"

She eyed the small bowl of green paste. "That I've tried. And my sinuses are sufficiently clear already, thank you."

He grinned. "I thought you said you were feeling adventurous. Mix a tiny bit with some soy sauce, then dip a piece of the spider roll into it."

She gave him a suspicious look before she poked the tip of a chopstick into the wasabi paste, gathering a small dollop onto the stick. She transferred the wasabi carefully into the bowl of soy sauce and stirred. "You must think I'm a complete rube."

He grinned. "Not many sushi places in Purgatory."

"Not *any* sushi places in Purgatory," she corrected. "Although I'll have you know, I have actually left the Purgatory city limits a time or two. I went to college, you know."

"And never tried sushi?"

"I didn't have any money to eat out while I was

in college." He saw her steal a glance at the diners at the next table, who were using their chopsticks like old pros. She picked up her own chopsticks and positioned her fingers on the sticks with fierce concentration as she maneuvered one of the pieces of spider roll between the two sticks. "I ate a lot of ramen, soup and crackers."

"The poor-student diet," he said with a nod. "I remember it well."

She grimaced as the chopsticks slipped, dropping the piece of sushi back to her plate. "Damn it."

He picked up the fallen piece of sushi with his own chopsticks, dipped it in the wasabi–soy sauce mixture and held it out to her. "Don't want you to starve."

Pinning him with a look that sent delicious shivers down his spine, she opened her mouth for the piece of spider roll. He leaned closer, watching with interest as she took her first bite.

Her eyes widened as she chewed, the touch of wasabi bringing tears to her eyes. But the look of surprise quickly shifted to pleasure that made the room seem suddenly warm and very, very close.

"You like?"

She nodded. "Wow. I don't know what I was expecting but that's amazing."

"Well, it's fried crab, so you can't really go wrong."

Her toothy grin in response was pure sunshine, heating up the atmosphere around him until he swore he felt sweat trickling down his back despite the blast of air-conditioning blowing overhead.

She waved her chopsticks at him. "So, what's the trick with these?"

Throwing caution to the wind, he reached across the small table and closed his fingers over hers, guiding them around the thin wooden sticks until they were positioned correctly. "Now tuck your middle finger under the top stick and use it to control the sticks."

She gave him a doubtful look.

Reluctantly, he let go of her hand and nodded. "Try it."

She positioned the chopsticks over the next piece of sushi and brought the sticks together to pick it up. It wobbled in the air as she stared at the rice-covered roll of fried crab as if she could hold it in place with the sheer force of her will.

Hell, maybe she could. She'd already wrapped him around her little finger without even trying.

Then the sushi roll dropped with a plop into the small bowl of soy sauce. "Damn it!"

He fished it out with his own chopsticks and put it on her plate again. "I won't tell anyone if you just eat with your hands."

She shot him a baleful look as she took another stab at the sushi with her chopsticks. "I will not let two little sticks defeat me."

This time, she maneuvered the roll to her mouth. Pleasure mingled with sheer relief as she chewed and swallowed.

"You're probably wishing you'd just opted for

the Reuben at the place across the street by now, aren't you?" he asked, picking up a piece of the salmon skin roll he'd ordered for himself.

"No," she said, not looking away from the next piece of sushi she had targeted with her chopsticks. "Anybody can pick up a sandwich and shove it in her mouth. Child's play."

"You know children in some countries start out learning to eat with chopsticks," he murmured.

The look she sent his way could have melted paint off the wall.

She wasn't a quitter—he'd give her that. By the time she reached the end of her spider roll, she was able to pick up the last piece, dip it in the wasabi-flavored soy sauce and pop it into her mouth with competence if not expertise. Swallowing the last bite, she grinned at him, triumph shining in her blue eyes. "Ha! Take that, chopsticks."

He grinned back at her, wondering why some other man hadn't already spotted this shining diamond of a girl and snatched her up—and wishing like hell that man could be him.

But it couldn't. For a lot of reasons.

"What's wrong?" she asked.

He realized his grin had faded to a frown. He straightened his expression. "Nothing."

Her eyes narrowed. "You went from smiling to scowling in about a second. What were you thinking about?"

"What's waiting for you back at the hospital," he answered. It was only half a lie; Danny's behavior earlier was a stark reminder of the first seventeen years of his life. Including the formative years—wasn't that what the shrinks called the first three years of a child's life?

His had been spent with a terrified mother who regularly took verbal and sometimes physical abuse to keep his father from touching him. And after she'd died of an aneurysm when he was five, there'd been no more buffers between him and the cruel, vicious monster his father became when he was drinking.

"Danny isn't always like that. Before he started drinking so much, he was a lot of fun." Absently playing around with the chopsticks, maneuvering them between her fingers as if she were practicing their use, she looked up at him with a wistful smile. "When we were younger, we were each other's favorite playmate. My mom was the poster child for bad decision-making, so we spent a lot of time hiding in the room we shared, making up games and pretending to be other people so we stayed out of whatever drama she was into that week. Danny was a couple of years older, but he was so patient with me. He never treated me like I was a pest, even when I was."

No wonder she was so protective of her brother. "I get it."

"Do you?" Her brow furrowed with a look of pure skepticism. "Do you have any brothers or sisters?"

"No," he admitted, wondering if his childhood would have been better or worse if he had. Dealing with the old man by himself hadn't been fun, and logic would suggest sharing his father's wrath with other siblings would have been something of a relief.

But would it have? Ginny's agony over her brother suggested that sharing the misery with a brother or sister would have multiplied the pain rather than divided it.

"I guess I don't get it," he admitted. "Not really. I mean—I can understand what you're dealing with intellectually, but—"

"But it's not the same as experiencing it."

"No."

She reached across the table, covering his hand with hers. Her touch was warm and soft, making him wonder what it would be like to feel her hands elsewhere. He crushed that thought ruthlessly. She wasn't the kind of girl who could see sex as purely recreational, and that was the only kind of sex he intended to have. Relationships, happily-ever-after—those were things other men could indulge in if they dared.

He knew what it was like when the happiness died and all that was left was the endless ever-after.

Chapter Nine

Rain had starting falling during the drive back to Purgatory, the relentless drumbeat of water on the windshield conspiring with the rhythmic cadence of the windshield wipers to lull Ginny perilously close to slumber by the time Anson parked in the alley behind the bakery.

"I don't have an umbrella with me, so we're going to have to make a run for the back door," Anson warned as he cut the engine.

"You go ahead," she muttered, settling deeper into the passenger seat. "I'll just sleep here."

She felt his hand on her arm, big and warm. "Come on, sleepyhead. Nice soft bed inside."

"Probably already occupied by another one of

your freeloading cousins," she murmured before she thought better of it. As soon as the words spilled from her lips, she sat upright, her eyes snapping open. "I am so sorry. That was incredibly rude."

He laughed as he unbuckled his seat belt. "Maybe, but it was pretty funny, too. And lucky for you, I don't have any other cousins."

She unbelted herself as well, trying to peer through the streaming rain sheeting against the windshield. "Nice night, huh?"

"Should make it easy to sleep," he murmured, slanting a look her way. "You want to stay here and let me go get an umbrella?"

She shook her head. "I won't melt."

He gave her a heated look that threatened to make a liar out of her before he opened the door. Rain needled its way through the opening, glittering his face with droplets of moisture. "Ready?"

She opened her door. "Ready."

They ran for it. Even with the added obstacle of having to run around the car, Anson caught up with her by the time they reached the narrow awning over the back door to the bakery. But his added speed didn't spare him from the same drenching that had her dripping and shivering as she waited for him to unlock the door.

"Brr," she said with a laugh, dodging the water dripping from his wet hair as he put the key into the lock. "So much for summer coming early this year."

"It'll be blazing hot soon enough," he promised, ushering her through the unlocked door. He shot her another warm look. "Bikini weather."

Was he flirting with her? She wasn't the world's best at discerning male interest, having spent most of her early life considering man-woman relationships—men in general, really—as unnecessary complications in her already-complicated life. Her mother's track record with men had been abysmal, hardly something Ginny had wanted to emulate. And Dolly Coltrane certainly hadn't known how to steer her daughter through the land mines of dating when she was old enough to feel the first stirrings of sexual attraction.

"Come on," he said, a smile flirting with his lips as he caught her hand and pulled her toward the stairs to the loft level. His fingers lingered briefly against hers before he let go and sent her up the stairs ahead of him.

The loft was blessedly free of unexpected visitors when Anson unlocked the door and let them in. He took a quick walking tour of the space just to be sure, coming back to where Ginny stood by the windows with a broad grin animating his lean, handsome face. "No cousins, no long-lost aunts or uncles, no strays—"

"Except for me." Self-consciously, she finger-combed her damp hair away from her face, fairly certain she must look as bedraggled as a lost kitten left out in the rain.

"Lucky for you, I'm a sucker for strays." For a moment, he lifted his hand toward her, as if he were going to help her tame the rain-curled chaos of her hair. But he dropped his hand back to his side and walked past her to the window. "Rain's not supposed to let up until midmorning."

She felt a sharp pang of disappointment that she quelled with ruthless discipline. "Like you said, good sleeping weather."

He turned to look at her. "Why don't you go get some dry clothes on and get to bed? I'll lock up."

"Dry clothes sound good," she admitted, peeling off her rain-drenched denim jacket. "Where should I put this to dry?"

He crossed and took the jacket from her hands, his fingers brushing hers in the process. Sparks flew. Literally.

He laughed. "Sorry about that. Static electricity."

Some sort of electricity that had nothing to do with friction jolted through her nervous system when he didn't immediately move away. She looked down at his hands, at the long fingers curled around the wet denim, then let her gaze move slowly upward, past the broad shoulders and sinewy neck to the strong, square jawline and incongruously beautiful lips.

Those lips parted on a shaky exhalation. Her name came out in a raspy whisper. "Ginny."

She met his gaze. His eyes were more black than brown, his pupils dilated in the low lamp-light.

"I don't know how to do this," she murmured.

His eyes twitched at her soft words, but he didn't pretend he didn't understand what she meant. "You don't have to do anything."

She shook her head. "I know I don't. I just—" She sighed, frustrated by her own hesitation, by the paralyzing awkwardness she felt around men in general and attractive men in particular.

The Gates was full of attractive men, virile and handsome men, and most of the time, she was happy that none of them seemed to notice her unless she was forced to bring herself to their attention in some work-related situation.

But Anson was different. He'd paid attention to her, looked beyond her role at the office to consider the person inside. That he'd begun to suspect her of being the mole at The Gates wasn't exactly flattering, of course, but it was better than ignoring her altogether, wasn't it?

Would you listen to yourself, Ginny Coltrane? Are you so desperate to be noticed by a man that you'd contemplate setting yourself up for a felony?

She couldn't stop a little bubble of laughter from escaping her lips at the thought.

Anson's brow furrowed. "Did I say something funny?"

Unfortunately, his confusion only made her laugh harder.

He took an uncertain step back from her, and she tried to get her nerves under control enough to at least keep from convincing him she'd lost her mind. "I'm sorry," she said, swallowing another giggle. "It's just—"

"The thought of anything happening between us finally sank in?" he asked, his voice light. But she was beginning to be able to read him after so many hours in his company.

She put her hand on his arm, closing her fingers around the surprising muscles that lurked beneath his shirt. "I was laughing at myself," she confessed, realizing that the only way she and Anson could get through the next couple of days working together to protect Danny was to just get her neuroses out there in the open so he'd know exactly what he had to deal with. "I was thinking how nice it was you ever bothered to look twice at me, even if it took suspecting me of leaking information to make you do it. It's the most attention I've gotten in forever. And then, *that* thought was so very sad that I had to laugh at myself about it. That's all."

His expression softened. "I noticed you a long time ago. Long before this internal investigation."

Her smile faltered. "What? Why?"

"Because you have a smile like sunshine. You don't use it often at work, but when you do, it's dazzling." Anson dropped her jacket on the coffee table and took a step closer to her, forcing her to look up at him to hold his gaze. He reached up and cradled her face between his large palms, his voice low and rough-edged. "I find myself looking at you even when I shouldn't. Like now."

A delicious shiver ran through her at his touch. "Anson, I'm really not very good at this."

"This?" He bent slowly, brushing his lips against hers. Just the lightest of touches, a soft caress, but it sent tingling sparks floating through her. He drew back from her, a faint smile curving the corners of his lips. "That wasn't so bad, was it?"

"No," she admitted. "But—"

His smile faded and his expression went unexpectedly serious. Dropping his hands away from her face, he took a step back. "I know this isn't the right place or time for anything more than friendship. You don't have to worry about that."

It was stupid of her to feel disappointed by his retreat. She hadn't wanted the complication, had she? Their relationship was already a tangle of conflicting loyalties, uncertain agendas and fragile trust.

And yet, the feel of his lips brushing hers lingered, a tangible memory of how much she had wanted him, in that moment, to finish what he'd started.

She took a deep breath and pasted on a smile. "Thank you for everything you've done for me in the past twenty-four hours. I don't even know how to begin to pay you back for it."

"No payback necessary." He waved his hand toward the large wall that screened off the bedroom. "Go get some sleep. Everything will make more sense in the morning."

Retreating to the bedroom, she finished stripping off the rest of her wet clothes and changed into fresh underwear and the large cotton nightshirt Anson had packed for her. Nestling beneath the blankets of his bed, she curled into a ball and listened to the sounds of Anson settling himself onto the sofa in the front room.

He was such a different man than she'd thought him to be. When she'd thought of him at all.

And now, just a day later, he seemed to be all she could think about.

WHAT THE HELL had he been thinking, kissing her?

Anson dropped his head back against the sofa cushion and stared at the rain-streaked windows refracting light from the streetlamps outside. Hadn't he decided that anything beyond friendship with a woman like Ginny Coltrane was trouble waiting to happen?

You never could resist trouble, Daughtry.

He closed his eyes, trying not to feel the softness of her mouth beneath his. Or the vulnerable look in her eyes when she'd gazed up at him, her expression full of questions he couldn't answer.

On the coffee table, his cell phone vibrated against the scuffed wood. He checked the caller ID. Marty Tucker.

He answered. "What's up, Tuck?"

"I'm hearing strange things here in mission control."

Anson glanced at his watch. After nine. Surely Tuck wasn't still at work. "You calling from the office?"

"Superspy has us working long hours." Tuck lowered his voice to a conspiratorial whisper. "On the upside, Bombshell Barbie is still here, too, and she's wearing that little blue number that makes her legs look ten miles long."

"She could probably snap your neck with those legs," Anson warned.

"I'm countin' on that, son." Tuck laughed. "Seriously, I'm hearing you took a beating for that mousy little blonde in Payroll?"

Anson frowned. "Ginny Coltrane. And I just got scuffed up a little." He pressed the bruise under his eye, grimacing at the pain. "No big deal."

"I didn't know you even knew the girl."

"It was a chance meeting."

"Someone tried to mug her or something?"

"Something like that." He reached for the laptop computer sitting on the coffee table and lifted the cover. His log-in page popped up and he typed in his password. "You just calling for the gossip?"

"You know me. I like to be in the loop."

"Well, now you know."

"I still don't know why we're suddenly burning the midnight oil trying to track down some guy in the BRI."

Ferris Bellander, Anson thought. One of the guys who'd attacked him at the Whiskey Road Tavern. "Quinn didn't say?"

"Not to me. But since it came on the heels of your heroic ass-kicking, I was kind of wondering if there was a connection."

"Beats me," Anson lied. "I'm on the disabled list, remember."

"Come on, you took a beating and the cavalry has suddenly mobilized, and you're telling me you don't know anything about it?"

"I'm saying, someone there at The Gates is more likely to give you the whole scoop than I am. And speaking of my heroic ass-kicking, it's time for me to get some shut-eye. I'm a little beat."

Tuck groaned at the bad joke, but it seemed to distract him from his questions, as Anson intended. "Okay, man, you clearly need some sleep if you can't come up with a better pun than that."

"Try not to work too hard."

"No chance of that," Tuck said with a laugh before he hung up.

Anson set down the phone and pulled up his email program to see what had come in while he'd been out of pocket. Not much of interest. A few emails from some programmer groups he was part of, a gaming thread that he hadn't really participated in for years but couldn't seem to quit out of nostalgia and a recent email from his cousin, Nicki, from this afternoon. He opened that one to see what she had to say for herself.

So sorry for this morning. If I'd known you were entertaining a woman, I'd have found somewhere else to crash. But since when do you entertain women?

Anson grimaced. "I'm not a eunuch, Nicki." The email continued.

She's pretty. Kind of normal for you, though, isn't she? Anyway, dropped by the office and applied for a job. Fingers crossed!

Surely Quinn wouldn't really hire Nicki, would he? He was bluffing. Messing with Anson's head. His cousin was the wildest of wild cards. Sending her undercover with the Blue Ridge Infantry would be pure folly.

Wouldn't it?

"I can't sleep."

The sound of Ginny's raspy voice sent electricity pulsing along his nerve endings. He turned to find her standing a few feet away, her arms wrapped around herself as if she were cold. The long T-shirt fell to midthigh, revealing several inches of toned leg that Anson had never seen before.

He tried not to stare. "Are you hungry?"

She shook her head.

"Thirsty?"

Her lips curved slightly. "No. I'm fine. I'm just wide-awake."

So was he, now. Ginny in her short nightshirt with messy bed hair was doing all sorts of electric things to his nervous system. "You could watch TV if you want."

She nodded at his open computer. "I'm disturbing you."

He shook his head quickly, in no hurry for her to leave him alone again, even though he knew he was playing with fire. "I was just checking email. All done."

She crossed to the sofa and sat beside him, keeping a small, safe distance between them. She looked down at her bare knees and blushed, tugging the hem of the T-shirt down as far as it would go. "I didn't have a robe."

"Are you cold? I could find something—"

As he started to rise from the sofa, she caught his arm. "I'm not cold."

He looked down at the small hand lying on his

arm. She had pretty hands, with long fingers and short, unvarnished nails. She dropped her hand away, but the warm feel of her fingers on his skin lingered.

"I have to tell you something." A hint of reluctance tinted her low voice, and she clasped her fingers together tightly in her lap. "About Mara Jennings."

Anson turned to look at her, his gut tightening. "You're not about to tell me—"

Her gaze snapped up to meet his. "That I'm the mole? No."

"Then what?"

"I was thinking about what you said. About why you suspected me." She looked down at her clasped hands. "I did guess a lot about Mara. That she was working on a special project. And that her sudden departure from The Gates was connected with that Colombian gunrunner that was killed near Deception Lake last month."

He didn't confirm anything, but he didn't suppose he needed to.

"The fact that the two people who were suspected were you and Nick Darcy told me two things. One, that Mara had been involved in some sort of international incident. Darcy's State Department background suggests that much. He always seems to end up in the middle of cases where there's an international element."

"Not the case that got him reinstated," Anson countered, a little unnerved by how much Ginny had guessed about the woman everyone at The Gates knew as Mara Jennings.

"Ah, but that was personal," she said with a little smile. "The woman he loves needed his help."

"And another one bites the dust," Anson murmured.

She cut her eyes at him. "Cynic."

He just smiled.

"Your involvement," she continued, "suggests there's a computer element to Mara's story. Maybe she was doing some computer work for Quinn. Something he wanted to keep under the radar. It makes sense—we know that the BRI is tangled up with anarchist hacktivists we suspect may be planning some cyber terror attacks."

She was dangerously close to the full truth, he realized. "Or maybe I knew her before she came to The Gates."

She shook her head. "I did some looking into Mara Jennings's background after she disappeared without giving notice. I was curious. A little worried, too. She'd always been fairly nice to be me."

"Then you know Mara didn't know squat about computers beyond how to turn one on and point and click her way through a game of Solitaire."

"You're right. She didn't." Her gaze came up to meet his. "But her sister Mallory did."

Well, hell. Anson tried not to react, but he'd never had much of a poker face. The look in Ginny's eyes suggested that he still wasn't much good at hiding his thoughts.

"Mara died in the fire in Texas. Mallory, the computer genius, lived. And took her twin's identity to escape the Colombian gunrunners who killed her sister by mistake."

Good God, Anson thought, she'd figured it out almost completely.

"I don't know what her connection to the gunrunners was," Ginny admitted, rubbing her knees with her palms in an endearing show of nerves. "I guess that's maybe where Quinn and Darcy come in. Maybe she was tangled up with them in some way. I don't know. I just think that's why she disappeared. Because there are still people out there looking for her."

Anson passed his hand over his face. "Ginny— you realize you just made yourself a prime suspect in the leak investigation. If I tell Quinn what you just told me—"

"I'll tell him myself," she said quietly. "It might be enough to convince him to put you back on active duty."

"But you could be fired."

She frowned, looking away. "I'll deal with that if it happens."

"Your brother's out of work. You'd have trouble finding another job with a black mark against you—"

"You're not the mole, Anson."

"Are *you*?" he asked.

She jerked her head up, her expression sharp with indignation. "Of course not."

"Then you don't need to tell Quinn anything," he said flatly. "I'll be fine. I'll figure out a different way to clear my name."

"I swear, I haven't told anyone my suspicions," she said quickly. "Not a soul before now. I liked Mara. I wouldn't want anything to happen to her."

"You pieced it together so easily." He felt sick. "If you could do it—"

"Only someone in payroll would have figured it out," she said. "And I was the only one who ever dealt with Mallory's paychecks, except the accountant, and like you said he wouldn't have enough information to figure it out."

Which made Ginny the only person outside of

Quinn, Darcy or Anson who could have leaked the information to the tandem of terrorist groups who'd gone after Mallory Jennings just over a month ago, Anson realized.

Or did it? If Ginny had figured out what Mallory was up to at The Gates, could someone else have put the clues together, as well?

A ding on his computer interrupted his thoughts. New email.

He glanced at the sender's name—Amon. And the subject line was empty. Probably spam. But as he reached to zap the email to his trash box, Ginny murmured, "Amon…"

He looked at her. "Someone you know?"

"No, but that sounds really familiar for some reason." Her brow crinkled. "I think it's a crossword puzzle answer. The name of an ancient god or something like that?"

Didn't ring any bells with him, but instead of dumping the email, he took a chance and opened it.

There was a single line of type on the screen.

Back off now. Below the words, a photo had been inserted into the email.

Beside him, Ginny gasped.

His own gut tightened with horror.

There on the screen, the image dark, grainy but unmistakable, was a photo of Ginny Coltrane lying in his bed.

Chapter Ten

"How is that photo possible?" Ginny tried to keep the tremble out of her voice, but she wasn't having much luck, given how hard the rest of her was shaking. Anson had wrapped her in the nubby cotton throw that hung over the back of his sofa, but cold wasn't her problem.

Terror was.

She had followed Anson into the bedroom, unwilling to stay in the main part of the loft alone, even though he was only a few yards away.

He was looking at a laptop computer that sat on a sturdy steel-top table near the bed. "Son of a bitch," he muttered.

"What?" She tightened the throw around her shivering limbs.

"Someone hijacked my laptop. Used the webcam to grab that still." He stepped aside so she could see that the laptop—and the web camera at the top of the monitor—were angled perfectly to have taken the photo of her lying on Anson's bed.

"Well, make them stop!" Her voice rose in pitch. She tried to lower it again. "You know how to do that, right?"

He closed the laptop lid. "That's one way."

She couldn't stop a bubble of shaking laughter from escaping her throat. "What now?"

"I need to figure out how they got through my security. See what other information they were able to access."

She was glad he sounded as if he knew what to do, because she didn't have a clue. Her knowledge of computers centered more on using the programs they ran more than the nuts and bolts of the hardware itself. "What do they want you to back off of?"

He turned to look at her, his expression serious. "There are only two things I'm involved in doing at the moment. Trying to figure out who the mole at The Gates really is and trying to help you figure out who's targeting your brother. If I had to choose which one I think inspired that email, I'd say the former."

"You mean you think it could be the mole himself who sent you the email."

He nodded. "If he can access my files on my spare laptop, then he could possibly have done so at The Gates."

"And you had sensitive information about Ma—"

Anson pressed his fingers against her lips, quieting her. "Not here."

Did he think someone was still listening?

He bent close to her, whispering in her ear. "Say nothing else. I'll get Quinn to sweep this place for listening devices."

But they'd already said so much, she thought. They'd had a whole conversation earlier about her suspicions regarding Mara and Mallory Jennings. If the place were bugged—

He pressed his forehead to hers. "It's going to be okay. Get dressed and we'll get out of here."

"And go where?"

He smiled slowly. "You'll see."

"THIS USED TO be the cellar." Anson came to a stop in the middle of a hallway on the bottom floor of the Victorian mansion that now housed The Gates. The corridor was flanked by three doors on each side, with a seventh door at the far end.

Ginny took in the pale green walls, the simple tile floor and, most tantalizing of all, the doors. "Where do those go?"

Anson's smile was nearly as mysterious as the doors. "Open one and find out."

She crossed to the nearest door and put her hand on the knob. "If I open this, is something going to jump out at me?"

He pressed his hand against his chest, feigning dismay. "You have no faith in me."

"If something does jump out at me, and I survive, I will make you pay."

He grinned. "Just open the door."

She turned the knob and gave the door a push. It opened silently, the overhead lights of the main room illuminating just enough of the smaller chamber to reveal the foot of a bed.

She felt along the wall until she found a light switch and flicked it on. "It's a bedroom."

"Technically, a dorm room."

"Do agents sleep here or something?"

"Sometimes. Usually when a case requires them to pull an all-nighter."

She knew all-nighters happened often enough. She'd seen the overtime vouchers Alexander Quinn signed for payroll.

She stepped back into the main room and looked up at Anson. She lowered her voice. "I had no idea this was here. Are there any people sleeping here right now?"

"I don't think so, but we can check." He nodded at the laptop computer that sat on a narrow desk near the door. "Agents log in on that computer if they're using a room. The information goes on the server so that any agent can access the information if there's a break in the case and they need to contact the resting agent. You'd have no reason to know about it, though, since you're not an agent and don't have to work after hours as a rule."

"Right."

He typed in a few keystrokes and shook his head. "All yours."

She returned to the room she'd just left and sat on the edge of the twin bed. The mattress was firm, the way she liked it. "Are they all alike?"

He nodded. "I know it's not much. But there's a phone in each room, like the one on the nightstand there. So agents can be easily reached in case of an emergency."

"It's enough," she said with an approving nod, and his mouth curved in a smile. She gave him a considering look. "It was your idea, wasn't it? These dorm rooms?"

"Yeah. We considered full-size beds, given the size of some of the agents, but Quinn wanted six rooms, and the bigger beds would have taken up too much of the space."

"What made you come up with the idea?"

"Too many nights sleeping on the floor under my desk while on call."

"Oh, that's right. You and the other IT folks have to be on call sometimes during big cases."

"Yeah, we do." His brow furrowed. "Or did, in my case."

She had seen how much it had bothered him earlier, upon their arrival, to have to get a visitor's pass. "I think Quinn knows you're not the mole," she said quietly. "He just has to give the investigation due diligence."

"I know. I think that's what's frustrating. Being stuck on interminable leave until someone can prove I'm not a sneaky liar." He shrugged, straightening his expression and managing a slight smile. "Quinn gave me the go-ahead to use our facilities to do some diagnostics on my computer to see if I can find the source of the intrusion. Get some sleep." He nodded at the bed. "I'll be in the IT section if you need me."

"Okay." She smiled back at him. "Good luck."

He paused in the doorway. "I'm going to figure this out, Ginny. You don't have to worry."

His earnest expression made her want to jump up from the bed, wrap her arms around him and give him the biggest, fiercest hug she had in her. Then she looked into his dark eyes and saw a dark intensity that transformed all those sweet, melty feelings into molten lava that flowed like liquid fire through her veins.

Her skin felt too tight. Her pulse throbbed in her ears.

Anson took a step toward her before he stopped himself. "Call me if you need me."

And like that, he was gone.

She released a gusty breath and fell back onto the mattress. Looking up at the light fixture on the ceiling, she gathered two fistfuls of bedspread and counted slowly to ten until the humming electricity flowing through her limbs subsided into a low level buzz of energy.

So much for sleep, she thought.

She stepped out into the main room again, looking toward the closed door at the other end of the room. Anson had said that was a bathroom, hadn't he?

Did it have a shower, too?

She opened the door, flicked on the light switch and took a look. Pay dirt. Besides the toilet and a sink, there was a shower stall in one corner of the small bathroom.

Maybe a nice, hot shower would relax some of the tension tightening her muscles into knots.

EXCEPT FOR THE night-shift security guard who manned the front gate, Anson knew he and Ginny were alone in the office. Marty Tucker had left about ten minutes before they arrived, the guard had told him when asked. Anson supposed, despite the ignominy of having to sign in as a visitor, it was a show of trust on Quinn's part to allow him full access to the agency resources without another person present to make sure he wasn't making off with the company staplers.

He was running a diagnostics program he'd written on the laptop that should tell him how someone had been able to get through his layers of security to take control of his webcam, but it would take at least two more hours to finish going through all the data on the computer in search of any sort of alien code.

What he was going to do if the diagnostic program didn't find anything at all, he wasn't sure. Probably go through the registry line by line, looking for a clue.

And that would take a hell of a lot longer than two hours.

He shoved his chair back and got up to stretch his legs, feeling tense. On edge. Maybe he shouldn't have left Ginny alone down in the dorms. Sure, the place was locked up tight and there was a guard out at the gate to make sure no intruders got in. And it wasn't exactly as if they'd told anybody but Quinn their plans to come here to The Gates for the night.

But he didn't like the idea of letting Ginny out of his sight for very long, especially after getting that photo of her in his bed, warning him to back off. Because what he was doing right now was anything but backing off.

He walked over to the window of the computer section and looked out at the grounds of The Gates. The front yard was large and well manicured, a landscaped lawn and gardens hedged in by crape myrtle bushes that lined the fence flanking either side of the ornate black iron gates that fronted Magnolia Avenue. Anson had seen the view many times before in the glow of a full moon, the pale blue light casting mysterious shadows across the yard. But tonight's rain turned the view into a watercolor rendered in grays and charcoals.

He felt sorry for Dale Murdock, the security

guard manning the front gates that night when they'd arrived. The booth where he spent most of his time was waterproof, but his duty included hourly rounds of the property to make sure everything was secure.

The booth was empty now. Murdock must be on his rounds.

Except hadn't he been finishing up his rounds just a few minutes earlier when he'd checked in with Anson to make sure everything was okay?

Anson checked his watch. Fifteen minutes, to be exact. He shouldn't be out on rounds again for another thirty minutes or more.

He crossed to his desk and pressed the intercom button that fed into the guards' booth. "Murdock?"

There was no answer.

Murdock should be wearing a shoulder radio, but only Quinn had a two-way link to the guards on duty.

You're borrowing trouble, he told himself, crossing back to the window. Murdock was probably on his way back to the booth after a bathroom break.

Except he wasn't. The booth was still empty. And there was no sign of Murdock.

Where the hell could he be?

GINNY TURNED OFF the shower and wrung out her hair, shivering a little as the cool air of the bathroom hit her wet skin. Stepping out onto the bath mat, she grabbed the thick gray towel she'd pulled from the linen closet just inside the bathroom and wrapped it around her. She twisted her hair up in a second towel and looked for the T-shirt she'd brought with her into the bathroom.

It wasn't draped across the sink counter where she'd left it.

Frowning, she opened the bathroom door and looked out into the dormitory corridor. It was empty, just as she'd left it.

She took another quick look around the bathroom to make sure the shirt hadn't slid off onto the floor. It hadn't.

Tucking the towel more tightly around her, she walked down to the far bedroom where she'd left the rest of her things and opened the door. The first thing she noticed was the light was on. She knew she'd turned it off when she went to the bathroom.

Hadn't she?

Then she saw the T-shirt she'd taken with her into the bathroom, now lying on the foot of the bed.

Maybe she'd left it here. She'd meant to take it with her into the bathroom, but she was functioning on very little sleep and a whole lot of stress. Maybe she'd just thought she'd turned off the light. And maybe she only thought she'd taken the shirt with her into the bathroom.

She picked up the T-shirt and looked around the bedroom, goose bumps scattering up her arms and down her back. The room was empty and looked undisturbed.

Get a grip, Ginny.

She pulled clean underwear from her duffel

and dressed quickly, tugging on jeans and a different shirt. No way was she going to be able to sleep now. She might as well take advantage of being here at The Gates and catch up with some of the work that had probably stacked up while she was dealing with the attack on Danny.

She was halfway up the stairs to the main floor when she heard a soft thumping noise behind her. She froze in place, her pulse thumping wildly in her ears.

Gripping the handrail tightly, she turned and looked down the stairs.

There was nothing there.

She released a whoosh of breath and leaned against the wall of the narrow stairway, feeling like an idiot. This place was the most secure building in Purgatory, Tennessee. Even if someone could get past the security guard at the front gates, she and Anson had locked the doors behind them.

The exterior locks were electronic, requiring a code that only employees of The Gates had access to. In fact, Anson didn't even know the code—Quinn had changed it after he'd put Anson and Nick Darcy on administrative leave. Ginny had been the one to key in the code to the office.

So there was no way an intruder had made it past two levels of security to get into The Gates.

Was there?

She hurried up the rest of the stairs and emerged onto the ground floor, a few steps from the front door.

Which now stood open, rain sheeting through the opening.

She stopped short, staring at the open door.

"Murdock!" Anson's deep voice drifted through the open doorway from somewhere outside, nearly swallowed by the drumbeat of rain.

Ginny hurried to the doorway and spotted Anson coming toward her down the cobblestone walk. He was rain-drenched, his T-shirt clinging to his body, revealing surprisingly toned muscles for a man who spent his life on a computer.

Though what did she know about his life,

really? In so many ways, he was still a stranger to her.

He looked up and stopped as he caught sight of her. "What are you doing up here?"

"Couldn't sleep. You can't find Murdock?"

"He's not in the guard booth."

"Maybe he's on rounds."

Anson reached the steps and took them two at a time until he stood before her, dripping onto the wooden porch that wrapped around the front of the old house. "He was just on rounds twenty minutes ago. And I looked all the way around the house—no sign of him. I just checked the booth to see if he left a note."

"And?"

Taking care to keep his distance, Anson shook the water from his shaggy hair and scraped the tangled curls back from his face. "There are muddy footprints leading to and from the booth, but also some impressions that might be drag marks."

Ginny shivered. "Drag marks? You think someone did something to Mr. Murdock and, what? Hid his body?"

"Maybe. We should call Quinn." Putting his hand on her shoulder, he gave her a nudge back inside the office and closed the door behind them, plunging the main lobby into darkness again.

Instinctively, Ginny took a step closer to Anson. He rubbed her back soothingly. "We should be safe enough in here—"

"You left the door open while you were out. Anyone could have come in while you were on the other side of the house." She thought about the strange things she'd encountered in the basement dormitory and shuddered again. "Anson, I think someone was in here. Maybe still is."

He listened as she told him about the missing T-shirt and how she'd found the lights on in her room. "You could have just forgotten," he said, but she could hear the doubts in his voice.

"I think we need to get out of here. We can call Quinn from the car."

He nodded. "I need to get my computer—"

"Let's just wait until we talk to Quinn."

"We can't," Anson said firmly. "If there really is someone in here, it might be the same person who breached my computer. And if so—"

"They'll try to destroy the evidence," she finished for him, understanding. "Okay. But we don't leave each other's sight."

"Agreed." He enfolded her hand in his own, his fingers gripping tightly as they hurried up the stairs to the second floor. As they reached the landing, Anson muttered a soft curse.

"What?" she asked, peering down the dark corridor.

"The light in the hallway was on when I went out to check on Murdock."

Ginny crossed to the wall switch and gave it a flick. The lights came on, spilling golden light down the hallway and revealing a series of closed doors on either side, save for one door that stood open near the far end.

"I closed the door to the computer room," Anson whispered.

"We should just get out of here."

He shook his head, his expression queasy. "I have to look."

As he started to pull away from her, she grabbed his hand. "Not by yourself."

He gazed down at her, wet curls flopping onto his forehead. He reached into his pocket and pulled out his keys, placing them in her free hand. "If you see anyone at all, you run for it, you hear me? Get out of here. Take my car and go. Call Quinn and call the sheriff's department. In that order."

She took a deep, shaky breath, closing her fingers tightly around the keys. She nodded toward the open door.

They walked, hand in hand, to the door and looked inside.

The computer section was empty. But it wasn't undisturbed.

His laptop computer was gone.

Chapter Eleven

"I logged the diagnostics program to the cloud, but if our computer thief was smart, he might have figured that out and found a way to delete the record." Anson Daughtry's deep voice rumbled with misery as he paced in front of Quinn's desk, looking like a rumpled, sodden mess.

Ginny Coltrane, on the other hand, looked clean and composed sitting in one of the two chairs across from Quinn, though the bleak look in her soft blue eyes gave away her tension.

Quinn directed his next question to her. "You're certain you took the shirt with you to the bathroom and turned off the light in the dorm room?"

She met his gaze steadily. "Yes."

Quinn's gut tightened unpleasantly. If both Ginny and Daughtry were telling the truth, an intruder had breached the walls of The Gates without setting off an alarm.

A quiet knock on his door drew his attention away for a moment. "Come in."

Adam Brand entered, looking grim. "We found Murdock. He's alive but unconscious. No signs of trauma, but we've called paramedics. Solano and Ava are giving him first aid."

Almost on cue the sound of sirens cut through the percussion of rain falling outside.

"Where was he?" Daughtry asked.

"Off the property, in the alley behind the drugstore. We think he was dragged there and hidden behind the trash bins." Brand sounded calm enough, but fury blazed in his sharp blue eyes.

Brand had suggested Dale Murdock for the job. Recently retired from the Bitterwood Police Department, still young at fifty-eight, Murdock had been looking for a night-shift job to correspond with his wife's shift at the hospital in Maryville.

He had a spotless record with the police department and had been a stellar employee since he'd started.

It was bad enough knowing that someone had rendered him unconscious and dumped him in the alley.

Worst of all was knowing the perpetrator had almost certainly been someone who worked at The Gates.

"Who's guarding him?"

"Fitz and Culpepper are standing watch. The sheriff's department investigators are on the way. The rest of us have done a search of the building from top to bottom. The intruder got away before Daughtry could sound the alarm."

Daughtry muttered a succinct profanity.

"You're back on active duty." Quinn looked at his IT director. "As of now. You have a hell of a lot of work ahead of you."

Daughtry didn't look surprised. He was smart enough to understand the implications of what had happened tonight. "On it."

Quinn looked at Ginny, taking in her messy hair, scrubbed-clean face and grim expression. "I assume you know what the events of tonight mean."

Ginny nodded soberly. "The intruder works here. Right?"

Quinn nodded. "When Daughtry went to your rescue the other night at the Whiskey Road Tavern, he got twisted up in someone's plan. We have to figure out what the plan could be—and who's behind it. And that means we may need to put some pressure on your brother."

Ginny blanched. "He's in the hospital."

"I have no intention of coddling a man who had enough cocaine hidden in his drawer to earn him a long time in prison," Quinn snapped.

"Quinn—" Daughtry stopped pacing, planted his hands on Quinn's desk and leaned toward him, fire blazing in his dark eyes.

Quinn raised an eyebrow. "Would you like me to tell the police what you did with that cocaine?"

Daughtry's brows converged over his long

nose. "Would you like me to tell the police who cleaned up after me?"

Quinn raised the other eyebrow, but Daughtry didn't budge.

Interesting.

Quinn turned his attention to Ginny, who sat straight-backed and alert in the seat. "We will take Mr. Coltrane's condition into account when we speak to him. But it has to be done."

"I want to be there," Ginny said.

Quinn shook his head. "That's not going to happen."

Ginny stood up, crowding Daughtry out of the way as she planted her small hands on the desk just as Daughtry had done. The self-contained, mousy payroll clerk of his experience was gone.

The kitten had claws.

"I will tell my brother not to cooperate unless I'm there. Understood?"

Quinn stood. Watching his employees exercise their spines was entertaining, but he was through indulging them. "He will manipulate your feelings until you interfere with our ability to get real answers from him. It will only slow down our investigation and put his life—and yours—in danger. Mr. Daughtry's, as well. Is that what you want?"

Ginny's nostrils flared and her jaw worked, but she stepped back and sat again, her spine rigid with suppressed fury. Daughtry, on the other hand, remained standing, his arms folded across his broad chest. He hadn't changed clothes yet, his damp clothing sticking to his body, revealing more muscle definition in his lanky body than Quinn had realized.

Maybe he needed to rethink Daughtry's value to the agency. Beyond his considerable computer skills, he'd shown a surprising level of physical bravery over the past couple of days. How much of that courage was due to his obvious desire to protect Ginny Coltrane from danger, Quinn wasn't certain. But it was an attribute that could be honed and utilized.

"Do you have something to add?" he asked Daughtry.

Daughtry shook his head, turning away.

"We'll be in touch," Quinn said, nodding to Adam Brand. "The safe house is ready?"

Brand nodded.

"Safe house?" Ginny asked.

"Your home isn't secure. Nor is Mr. Daughtry's. Clearly, we have a security breach here at the office, as well." Quinn quelled his own simmering rage at the thought of the failure of security at the office. He'd been too trusting of the men and women he'd hired, he supposed. A revision of security protocols was already in the works.

"I can return to the hospital and stay there," Ginny suggested.

"You're not safe at the hospital, either," Daughtry protested, turning to look at her.

Some silent message flowed between the two of them as they locked gazes. Finally, Ginny's gaze dropped to her clasped hands. "I'll need to pick up some more things."

"Already taken care of," Quinn told her.

Her gaze narrowed as she focused on him. "Any other part of my life you'd like to control while you're at it?"

Quinn didn't let himself smile, though he felt sorely tempted to. Ginny Coltrane continued to surprise him, and while he didn't normally care for surprises, her unanticipated combination of intelligence and fire could definitely be an asset to The Gates.

But not if he drove her off, he reminded himself. She'd have to be handled with finesse.

"Returning to your home after a breach only puts you in unnecessary danger," he said in a conciliatory tone. "Our agents were there already. We packed a few things you'll need over the next week or so."

"My computer?" she asked.

"Also packed."

Her eyes narrowed further. "Makeup, toiletries, tampons?"

He suppressed another smile. "A female agent

was tasked with selecting the things you might need."

"What about *my* toiletries?" Daughtry drawled.

Quinn slanted a hard look at him.

Daughtry shrugged and walked away, moving to the window that looked eastward toward the mountains. The view was obscured by rain and darkness, rendering the window a mirror that reflected his troubled expression.

"Brand, take Ginny and reacquaint her with her things. Daughtry, I need to speak to you alone."

Daughtry turned to watch Ginny Coltrane leave the office with Brand. Only when the door closed behind them did he turn his gaze to Quinn. "Do you have any suspects?" Daughtry asked.

"Everybody in this agency. Except you and Darcy." Quinn rubbed the back of his neck, feeling old. "You and Ms. Coltrane will have to talk to the sheriff's department investigators before you leave for the safe house. Meanwhile, Olivia Sharp is in the computer section, gathering what you'll need to do your work off-site. You don't need to come back here to get your job done—I don't want to risk your life any more than I want to risk Ginny Coltrane's."

"I can take care of myself."

"I realize that. I'm trusting you to take care of Ginny."

Daughtry's eyes narrowed. "Aren't we going to have guards at the safe house?"

"Of course. But you can provide an extra layer of protection."

Daughtry shook his head. "I'm not an agent, Quinn."

"I know you're not. But you've shown me you're capable of a lot more than I've asked of you. And you're motivated."

"What's that supposed to mean?"

Quinn finally allowed himself a smile. "You're a smart man. Figure it out." He looked down at his desk, dismissing Daughtry.

His newly reinstated IT director remained where he was for a long moment. Quinn could feel the full weight of Daughtry's gaze on him, but he didn't look up. He would indulge an agent's show of rebellion only so far.

The Gates had one boss. Quinn was it.

Finally, Daughtry walked away, his gait brisk with barely leashed anger. The door slammed behind him as he left.

Quinn leaned back in his chair and released a long, frustrated sigh. So neither of his prime suspects was the mole. Not that he'd ever really believed they were. But there was still someone inside The Gates who was willing to put lives in grave danger for his or her own agenda.

Quinn had to find the mole soon, before everything he'd worked so hard to build came crashing to the ground, burying them all.

"QUINN ALWAYS GETS his way, doesn't he?"

Anson looked up to find Ginny standing in the open door of his room at the safe house, her expression troubled. She was still wearing the jeans and T-shirt she'd put on back at The Gates, but she'd kicked off her shoes, baring clean pink toes tipped with dark blue nail polish.

He smiled at the sight, almost forgetting what she'd just asked. When those bare feet shifted position impatiently, he made himself look up to meet her gaze. "Yes, he does. Because he's generally right."

She didn't like his answer, he saw, her lips flattening to a thin line of annoyance. She entered the room and closed the door behind her, stopping a couple of feet from the bed, her arms crossing her chest. "He had no right to tell me I couldn't be there with Danny when he's questioned."

"You'd try to intervene."

"So?"

"So, Quinn and his agents know what they're doing. Some of them were cops. Feds. Hell, for all I know, some of them were CIA agents like Quinn before they started working at The Gates."

"And that makes it okay? They waterboard people, you know."

He squelched a smile at her indignant tone.

"I don't think they'll be waterboarding your brother."

"You don't know *what* they'll be doing, do you?"

"I know that they aren't sadists. And they're not going to do anything that would result in injury to your brother or lawsuits for the company."

Her expression went bleak. "Danny's in a lot of danger, too, isn't he?"

Anson held his hand out to her. "Sit down. Try to stop worrying."

She looked at his hand for so long he almost dropped it back to his side. But finally, she placed her hand in his and let him tug her over to the bed. He let go of her hand and patted the mattress next to where he sat with his back to the headboard. "Sit," he invited.

She sat on the edge of the bed.

"I don't bite. Much."

Her lips curving, she pulled her legs up onto the mattress and scooted closer. When he tucked her under his arm, she didn't resist. "I'm so tired."

"I know. You haven't had much sleep in the last two days."

"I try. I close my eyes but all I can see are those men surrounding me in the parking lot at the Whiskey Road Tavern."

He rested his head against hers. "You're safe here. Nobody at the office but Quinn, Brand and those two agents out there guarding us know where we are."

"Anson, even I know where we have safe houses."

"So do I," he admitted. "But did you pay attention on the drive here?"

She looked up at him. "Not really."

"I did. And this house is not on the list of safe houses I know about."

Her brow furrowed. "Are you sure?"

"Positive."

"Hmm." She pulled her knees up to her chest, folded her arms atop them and rested her chin on her forearms. "But Quinn is right—it had to be an inside job."

He laid his hand between her shoulder blades. "Yes."

She turned her head to look at him. "And we don't have a clue who it is, do we?"

"I have some thoughts," he admitted, though he wasn't ready to share his suspicions with anyone. Not even her. "But I've been on the wrong end of a false accusation. I'm not going to do that to anyone else until I have my facts in place."

The biggest problem, as far as he could see, was that so far the clues were contradictory. Whoever had sent him that photograph of Ginny had been able to mask his email address effectively. And clearly he had some computer savvy if he could somehow get past Anson's security to take over the web camera in his spare laptop.

There had to have been some sort of malware loaded onto his computer that his antivirus didn't catch. But how had someone managed to make that happen? Anson didn't accept files from people he didn't trust.

Which meant whoever had put the program on his computer was someone he'd trust enough to open a file that came from him. Or her.

"What are you thinking?" Ginny asked.

He realized he'd been woolgathering while she watched. "Just thinking about how someone was able to get past my security to load a program that would take over critical computer functions."

"Is that what happened?"

"I believe so. But that makes me wonder—" He rolled off the bed and crossed to the computers he'd set up earlier upon their arrival at the safe house. "If my spare laptop had the virus, then it had to have come through the network at The Gates. Because I don't get files through that laptop."

"What does that mean?" She pulled up the extra chair in the room and sat next to him, looking at the computer screen where he was pulling up a log of system errors from the past six months. "What are you looking for?"

"For the past few months, I've gotten errors from time to time—the network firewall picking something up—but the alerts were vague and they all seemed to resolve themselves. And then

I was put on administrative leave, and I didn't get to look into the problem any further."

"But?"

"But maybe whoever engineered the malware program that hijacked my laptop also has control of all the computers at The Gates. Which means he or she has access to everything. But while they managed to create a program that can fool most any antivirus program, they forgot to take the server firewall into consideration."

"Is that why you were getting alerts? The firewall was detecting the malware program?"

"That's my best guess."

"What did you do about the alerts? Did you ignore them?"

Anson looked at the computer screen, his gut tightening with dismay. "I assigned someone else to check into the alerts. I was busy with other things."

"What did that person discover?" she asked carefully, as if she sensed his reluctance to speak.

"I don't know." He turned to look at her. "I

was put on administrative leave before I got an update."

She caught his hand, closing her cool fingers around his. "Do you think that's how the information about Mallory Jennings got to the bad guys? Through the computer breach?"

He nodded, feeling sick. "I didn't catch the breach, and Mallory almost got killed, along with the man who was trying to protect her."

"There can't be that many people with the knowledge to create a program that could do what you're talking about, are there?"

"More than you'd think," he said quietly. "And a whole lot of them were working for the Wayne Cortland crime organization."

"Quinn's obsessed with mopping up what's left of Cortland's crew." Ginny's fingers were doing all sorts of shiver-inducing things to his hand, but if she realized what she was doing to him, she didn't show it. "But you know that, of course."

Anson nodded. Like everyone who worked at The Gates, he knew that bringing down the remains of Cortland's crime network was Quinn's passion. Too many people had been lost to those bastards already.

But they were like roaches, scuttling into corners and hidey-holes whenever a light was shone on them. Finding them all was proving to be an enormous task.

"So you think one of the hacktivists who was working for Cortland has somehow gotten past Quinn's background checks and found his way inside The Gates."

"I'm sure of it," he said.

He even had a pretty good idea who it might be, as much as he didn't want to believe it.

The problem would be trying to prove it.

"You *do* have a suspect, don't you?"

"I do. But I'm not going to say. Not until I know more."

She nodded slowly. "I get that."

The smell of her—soap, water and some indefinable essence that he'd come to recognize as Ginny—filled his lungs as she leaned a little closer to him. Did she have any idea just what the feel of her small, soft body tucked close to him was doing to him?

She turned her head toward him, her blue eyes soft. "I should go to my room now, shouldn't I?"

Maybe she did know.

"Yeah, you probably should." His answer was little more than a raspy exhalation. He waited for her to move away, dreaded it.

"I don't think I can," she murmured, her eyes darkening as she lifted her face toward his.

Oh, hell. He really, really shouldn't kiss her.

But he did.

Chapter Twelve

Ginny wasn't sure what she'd been expecting from Anson when he bent his head and touched his mouth to hers, but it wasn't this slow tease of a kiss, the brush of his lips across hers—once, twice, a third time, each touch lingering longer and longer until she parted her lips and invited more.

He slanted his mouth across hers, deepening the kiss, his tongue sliding over her lower lip before it delved inside to tangle with hers. His long-fingered hands splayed across her back, dragging her closer until she straddled his lap, her breasts pressing against the hard wall of his chest.

Desire licked low in her belly, so intense it

caught her off guard. She was no virgin, despite her outwardly composed demeanor, but she'd never been driven by passion, never come anywhere close to feeling consumed by volatile emotion. Caution had been her best line of defense against living a life as disastrous as her reckless mother's short, sad existence. Taking chances was something other people did, not Ginny.

But wrapped in Anson's arms, fire blazing through her veins with each touch of his hands on her body, she felt something inside her soul struggling to get out, like a butterfly frantically beating its wings against the chrysalis holding it captive.

The suddenness with which Anson closed his hands around her arms and pushed her away made her gasp. His molten brown eyes met hers briefly before he turned his head toward the sound of rapping on the closed bedroom door. "Yes?" he called.

"Quinn's on the phone for you" came a male voice from the other side of the door. That would be Jeff Benton, Ginny thought. The other guard assigned to the safe house was an Amazon of a redhead who'd introduced herself as Celeste Kuiper.

Anson looked at Ginny, regret in his eyes. "I have to take it."

She managed a smile. "I know."

"I'll be back. It's okay if you don't want to be here when I return."

Did she? she wondered as she watched Anson slip out the door, closing it behind him. If she was here when he came back, would they just go back to what they'd been doing before the knock on the door?

How far had they intended to take things tonight?

She scooted to the edge of the bed and put her bare feet on the nubby carpet, willing herself under control again. A lot of people saw sex as harmless recreation—her mother had been one of those people. But Ginny had seen how a little "harmless" fun could weigh on a person who, deep down, longed for happiness and commitment and forever.

She was one of those people. She'd known it as a small child, knew it ever more certainly now that she was a grown woman who'd tasted a little of the other kind of life. In college, she'd tried to conform to the hookup culture, though two partners in four years wouldn't exactly win her any prizes for conformity.

Everybody had told her sex was supposed to be fun, but all she'd seen was how it made her long for things that her partners were never going to offer her—closeness, commitment, friendship and, well, forever.

She didn't think Anson was the kind of guy who could give her those things, either.

Get up, Ginny. Get up and go back to your room. He'll have his answer and maybe you two can go back to just being Ginny from Payroll and Anson from IT.

She pushed to her feet and opened the bedroom door.

Anson stood on the other side, his expression grim.

She took a step back, her heart beginning

to thud hard against her breastbone. "What's wrong?"

"An orderly took Danny down for an X-ray an hour ago," Anson told her, closing the distance she'd put between them. He put his hands on her upper arms. "Our guards were told they couldn't go with them."

"What happened?"

"Danny and the orderly never came back."

"THEY FOUND THE ORDERLY, tied up but alive. The Knoxville police are debriefing him now. Our guys are being questioned, as well." Quinn's voice was calm over the phone, but Anson had worked with the man long enough to recognize a thread of worry in his tone.

"Did he say if Danny was hurt?" Ginny's face was pinched with worry, but to her credit, she was about as calm as Anson could have hoped for. Her hands were clasped together so tightly that her knuckles were bone-white, but she hadn't tried to race off to Knoxville after the first knee-jerk rush for the door.

"From what we've been able to glean, Danny didn't put up a fight, and the man didn't seem to treat him roughly."

Anson glanced at Ginny again. Her eyes were closed, her brow furrowed with dismay. He sighed. "You're thinking Danny was in on it, aren't you, Quinn?"

"I have to consider the possibility."

Ginny stood up abruptly and walked out of the kitchen. Benton and Kuiper both shot questioning looks at Anson. He got up and followed her. The two agents would brief him on anything else Quinn had to say.

He knocked on the door of the bedroom she'd been assigned. "Ginny?"

"You should be in there talking to Quinn. I'm fine."

He tried the doorknob and was relieved she hadn't engaged the lock. "I'm coming in."

"Anson—"

He ignored her protest and entered, finding her sitting cross-legged in the middle of the bed, the blanket wrapped around her. She shot him a baleful look but didn't say anything when he sat next to her on the bed. "I know this is hard, Gin."

Her lips curved slightly at his shortening of her name. "I don't even know my brother, do I? Not anymore."

"I don't know," he admitted, thinking of his own recent kick in the emotional gut. "People surprise you. Not always in good ways."

"I wish I could say I'm surprised. But I'm not. Not really." The pain and disappointment in Ginny's voice made Anson's heart hurt. But the way she was sitting, cocooned from the world outside her, didn't exactly invite him to offer her any physical comfort.

"Is there anything I can do for you?" he asked, feeling helpless and hating it. He'd spent most of his childhood and youth feeling completely impotent, unable to appease his father or escape his emotional cruelty. The experience had engendered in him a need to act, to do something, to change circumstances for the better.

But there was nothing he could do for Ginny at the moment. He could see that truth in her soft blue eyes as they met his.

"There is one thing you can do," she said after a long moment of tense silence.

"Name it."

"Go find the mole at The Gates. You said you had a suspect."

"Right," he said, trying to hide his dismay at the thought. He had a suspect, all right. A person he'd thought he could trust. Someone he liked.

"I'm going to try to sleep," she said, rolling onto her side with her back to him. A dismissal if he'd ever seen one.

He wanted to lie down beside her, tuck her body against his and hold her until she fell asleep. But he could tell Ginny wasn't ready to accept his comfort.

He rose from the bed and walked to the door. "I'll be next door. If you need me."

She didn't respond. He tried not to take it personally.

He needed sleep. But when he reached his room, he bypassed the bed and settled in front of the computer array he'd set up shortly after they arrived at the safe house. With the laptop stolen, he was left with trying to do a cybercrawl through the network at The Gates to see if he could ferret out the pesky malware offender that had caused all the trouble.

And then, see if he could track it back to his prime suspect.

He sat back with a sigh, his stomach aching. "Oh, Tuck," he murmured.

It had to be Marty Tucker. He was the one Anson had tasked with looking into the firewall alerts. He was one of the handful of people who could have sent Anson a file to download that he'd have opened without hesitation.

Maybe that was where he should start. With file attachments received just prior to the first logged alert from the network firewall.

He logged in to the network at The Gates through the safe house's secure Wi-Fi connection and started a system-wide search for every file or attachment downloaded into the system for a week prior to the first logged alert from the network firewall.

Then he leaned back in the chair and did a similar search through the memory cells of his own brain, trying to come up with any clue he might have missed that his trusted right-hand man, Marty Tucker, could be the mole at The Gates.

Tuck had been an old acquaintance from Anson's four-year crawl through the hallowed halls of Georgia Tech. Their paths had crossed less often than people might assume, given their identical majors. For one thing, Tuck had been two years ahead of Anson, already a junior during Anson's freshman year.

Tuck had also been more of a party animal. Despite Anson's reputation around The Gates as a free spirit, he'd taken his college education seriously. His degree was going to get him the hell off Smoky Ridge for good and allow him to see the world.

And it had, for a few years, until Alexander Quinn had called with an offer Anson had been unable to refuse.

Anson had been consulted when Tuck applied for the job in the company's IT department. Anson had given him a thumbs-up rating and in the year he'd been working with Tuck at The Gates, Anson had never had reason to doubt his assessment of the man.

Sure, Tuck could be irreverent and mercurial, but Anson had known few computer people worth a damn who hadn't honed a wicked sense of humor over the years.

He checked the search on the computer, a little surprised at how many downloads had shown up already. And the search was only 15 percent complete.

He made a mental note to discuss computer protocols with Quinn once he was back at his old desk in the IT office. But he supposed for now, it could wait until things with Ginny and her brother settled down.

Was Danny Coltrane still alive? Without anything else to go on, he had to assume that the mystery man who'd taken him out of the hospital was connected to the Blue Ridge Infantry, just as the man who'd stabbed him had been. But why hadn't they simply finished the job there at the hospital?

Had Danny convinced them he was more valuable to them alive?

Anson hoped so, for Ginny's sake.

A soft knock on his door drew his gaze away from the slow-moving progress indicator on his computer. "Anson?" Ginny's voice was faint from the other side of the door.

"Come in," he called.

The door eased open and Ginny slipped inside, her expression apologetic. "I couldn't sleep."

He turned his chair around to face her. "You need sleep."

"I couldn't turn off my brain."

"Worried about your brother?"

She nodded, crossing to sit on the end of his bed. She nodded toward the computer. "What're you doing?"

"Searching for the source of that malware I told you about." He rolled the chair closer to the bed until he sat right in front of her. "I think Danny's still alive."

She nodded, rubbing her hands over her knees in small, nervous circles. "Otherwise, they'd have killed him at the hospital and left him there for someone to find."

"Which I think means he probably managed to convince them he was more valuable to them alive." He put his hands over hers, stilling their restless movement. "Quinn has people looking for him. They know what they're doing. And the cops are looking, too."

She turned her hands so that her palms touched his, her fingers closing around the heels of his hands. "I'm really glad you're here."

"So am I." He lifted her hands, turning them so that he could press a light kiss against her knuckles. "I know I'm not exactly anybody's idea of Prince Charming—"

"I'm not looking for a fairy tale." She brushed the knuckles of one hand against his cheek before tugging her hands free. "To be honest, I'm really not looking for anything at all."

Ouch.

He rolled his chair back a few inches. "Okay. Message delivered."

She frowned, her brow furrowing over her soft blue eyes. "That isn't exactly what I meant. That is, I did mean it when I said I'm not looking for anything. I don't expect anything from you, just because you kissed me earlier. So you don't have to feel—" She cut off her words with a sharp sigh. "You know."

He wasn't sure he did. "You're saying you don't expect me to see what happened tonight as anything but some sort of aborted hookup?"

"I guess. Yeah."

"That's not how I saw it."

Her brow furrowed even further. "It's not?"

"Is it how you saw it?"

She sat back, consternation darkening her eyes. "I don't know that I really saw it as anything in particular," she answered carefully. "It was, um—"

He groaned. "Please, whatever you do, don't say *nice*."

She released a little huff of laughter. "It was… lovely."

"That might be worse than *nice*."

"No. You're a good kisser." Her gaze dropped to his mouth, and he felt his heart rate kick up a notch. "Soft and firm in all the right ways."

He tried to hide the leap of pleasure her words gave him. "I don't know whether it's appropriate to say thank you for that, but, thank you."

Her eyes snapped up to meet his, flashing with amusement. "I liked kissing you. I wouldn't mind kissing you again sometime."

"But not now?" he asked gently, reading the worry in her gaze.

"I want so badly to feel something besides terror right now. But I'm afraid I might make the wrong decision for the wrong reason, and I don't want to do that. I need you to understand that I came in here because I don't want to be alone. Not for any other reason."

"Understood."

She reached behind her and produced a deck of cards from her back pocket. "Remembered to pack these."

He grinned. "You gonna play strip Solitaire? That could be fun."

There it was. That pretty smile that felt like sunshine. "No stripping. And it doesn't have to be Solitaire. Do you have to supervise whatever your computer is doing over there?"

"You want to take me up on that game of Slapjack we never got to play, don't you?"

Her smile widened. "I do."

"You know I haven't had much sleep and my

reflexes are a little slow, right?" he asked as she scooted up the bed to make room for him. He tucked his long legs up cross-legged and waited as she dealt the cards.

"Oh, I'm counting on it," she assured him.

Anson hadn't played Slapjack since middle school, but there wasn't much to it, just an alternating dealing of cards until a jack appeared, at which point, the first to see it slapped his or her hand over the card and won all the cards that lay below.

He'd always been quick, but Ginny was quicker, her small hands darting out to claim the prize faster than he could react. She smoked him in two straight games before he finally held up his hands. "I surrender. You're the Slapjack champion of the safe house."

She gathered up the cards and shuffled them with the skill of someone who'd played a lot of hands of Solitaire. "Maybe you need a game that requires brains, not reflexes."

"Let me guess, Go Fish?"

She grinned again, as he hoped she would, and he basked in the warmth until her smile slipped, replaced by a little frown and a furrowed brow. "Do you think it's good or bad that we haven't heard anything new from Quinn?"

"I don't know," he answered honestly. "No news isn't bad news, is it?"

She shook her head quickly, setting the deck of cards on the bed between them. "At least it means they haven't found a body."

He reached across the space between them and took her hands. "I don't think those men are going to kill your brother, Gin. I think if they were planning to do something like that, they'd have killed him and left him at the hospital to be found by the authorities."

"I know you're right. But—"

"No buts. We don't deal in buts in this business."

She quirked an eyebrow at him. "Who says?"

"I do. And since I'm back on the job and

currently the senior-ranking employee in this room—"

Behind him, the computer made a soft ding.

"Hold that thought," he told her, sliding off the bed and settling in the desk chair in front of the computer. The search had finished, listing fifty-three files downloaded in the week before the firewall started throwing alerts at him.

"If I hadn't been suspended, I would have figured this out sooner," he said as he scanned the list of files. Some were word-processing documents, some were spreadsheets, some portable document files and image files. A few executable files, too. All of them were vulnerable to infection, yet the sophisticated internet security program that ran on the computers at The Gates hadn't caught anything.

Which possibly meant that whoever infected the system would have known the ins and outs of the company's antivirus program and knew how to circumvent its protection.

"My guess is that we're looking for some sort

of rootkit. I won't bore you with the details of what that means, but basically, we're looking for a program that would mask any attempts to infect the system with a virus. The end result would allow the user to get proprietary access to the system that would normally be available only to the system administrator. Which would be me." He reached into the backpack lying on the floor next to the computer and withdrew a flash drive. "But this flash drive is going to help me figure out just what kind of rootkit we're looking at. While I was on administrative leave, I spent some time working on a rootkit detection program. It's still pretty buggy, but I think it'll do what I want it to do. At least, I hope so."

As he inserted the flash drive into one of the computer's USB ports, he glanced over his shoulder.

Ginny was asleep, curled up on her side atop the blankets of his bed.

He finished loading the program and set it up

to examine the files he'd isolated, then turned back to the bed to look at Ginny. She had to have been exhausted by now. God knew he was, and he hadn't been under nearly the amount of emotional stress she'd experienced in the past couple of days.

He picked up the extra blanket that lay folded at the bottom of the bed and covered Ginny. She made a soft grumbling noise and curled into a tighter ball on the right side of his bed.

Leaving the left side empty and tempting as hell.

He glanced back at the computer screen. The program had barely ticked any progress. It might be an hour or two before it finished running through the processes he'd set up to detect malicious code in the files.

And that empty side of his bed was calling his name.

He eased himself onto the bed and stretched out next to Ginny, careful not to jostle her. Even so, she made another low mumbling noise and rolled onto her back, her head turning toward him.

Up close, she was impossibly pretty, even without a smidgen of makeup and her hair rumpled by the pillows. She had great skin, lightly dusted with tiny freckles across her nose and cheeks. Soft, pink lips the same rosy hue as the blush of color in her cheeks.

Yet somehow, she'd escaped the notice of most of the men at The Gates. Some of them weren't in the market, of course, but there were plenty who still were. They all managed to notice Olivia Sharp whenever she entered or exited a room, and while "Bombshell Barbie," as Tuck called her, was a fine-looking woman, was she any prettier than Ginny Coltrane?

Anson didn't think so.

In her sleep, Ginny sighed, rolling over to face him. He held his breath for a moment, until he reassured himself she was still asleep.

He would move soon. In just a few minutes.

Sometime later, he woke to a soft pinging

sound coming from his computer. With a start, he opened his eyes and found himself nose to nose with Ginny. He wasn't sure who'd made the move, him or her, but she was tucked into the curve of his body, so close his entire body seemed to go into pure sexual shock.

The computer alert dinged again. Anson turned his head to look at the computer screen, squinting a little to read the on-screen message window.

Malicious Software Detected.

He moved carefully away from Ginny's warm body, welcoming the cool air streaming up from the half-open window. Resisting the temptation to stand in the flow of air until his body stopped vibrating with desire, he settled into the desk chair and took a closer look at the infected file.

It was a spreadsheet file, one of several that ran through the network system in any given month. He'd expected the culprit to be something exactly like that—a file nobody would think twice about opening, himself included. But the source of the file wasn't at all what he'd expected.

The file name was February Payroll.

Anson looked over his shoulder at the sleeping woman on his bed, his gut twisting into a painful knot.

The malware-infected file had come from Ginny.

Chapter Thirteen

Alexander Quinn's cabin atop Laurel Rise had a magnificent view of the Smoky Mountains during the day, but at midnight, only a few scattered lights from mountain homes dotted the darkened landscape visible from his front porch.

He tightened his grip on the phone as he listened to Jeff Benton's succinct summary of the most recent events at the safe house.

"And Daughtry is certain?"

"He says so."

"Where is Ms. Coltrane now?"

"She's in his bedroom. She apparently fell asleep on his bed while he was working on the computer."

"Is Daughtry with her?"

"No, Kuiper is."

A breeze blowing across the ridge made Quinn pull his jacket more tightly around him. He supposed he could go inside the cabin to escape the sudden chill, but somehow, greeting this latest troubling news in the midnight gloom seemed more appropriate.

Ginny Coltrane, the mole?

He wanted to protest. He wanted to believe his gut instinct that she wasn't capable of that sort of treachery. That level of deceit.

She wasn't a computer expert. She'd never shown more than a moderate facility with technology of any sort.

But she was smart. A lot smarter than he'd given her credit for, he thought, remembering their discussion outside the hospital when she'd confronted him with questions about Anson Daughtry and his connection to Mallory Jennings.

Or maybe she'd known about Mallory Jennings because she'd managed to infiltrate the agency's computer network, including the top secret files that only Quinn, Daughtry and Nick Darcy should have been able to access.

"Where's Daughtry now?" he asked Benton.

"Outside, taking a walk."

"I need to talk to him. In person. If he's not back in ten minutes, go find him. I'll be there in twenty minutes."

He hung up without saying goodbye, already heading inside for his car keys.

"HAS SOMETHING HAPPENED?" Ginny asked, eyeing the tall, red-haired woman standing just inside Anson's bedroom door.

"I'm not sure," Celeste Kuiper answered calmly. "I was told to stay here and make sure you stay inside."

"Is that to protect me? Or keep me prisoner?"

Celeste arched a ginger eyebrow. "Why would you think I was keeping you prisoner?"

Ginny's gut squirmed. The other woman might

as well have admitted she was playing warden. "Where's Anson?"

"I'm not sure."

"Can you go find him?"

"That would be disobeying my orders."

"And if I decide to walk out of here?"

The other ginger eyebrow rose.

Ginny was tempted to try it, but Celeste was half a foot taller and had the lanky, rawboned look of an athlete. Ginny was in pretty good shape, but she was no match for a trained agent who outweighed her by thirty pounds of muscle.

She sighed and sat back down on the edge of the bed. "Okay, fine. Can you just tell me one thing—does this have anything to do with my brother? Has he been found?"

"I don't think so," Celeste answered, her drawl softening along with her hazel eyes. "I'm sure if anyone learned anything about your brother's whereabouts, they'd have told you first."

Ginny wasn't as sure.

A knock on the door made her nerves jangle, but Celeste looked unfazed. "Yeah?" she said.

"He's here," Jeff Benton said through the closed door.

"Got it," Celeste replied.

"Who's 'he'?" Ginny asked as Benton's footsteps receded down the hall.

"Quinn."

Of course it was Quinn. Anytime anything odd was going on these days, Quinn was right in the middle of it. "But you don't know what's going on?"

Celeste didn't answer.

"You *do* know what's going on."

Celeste remained silent.

"I want to see Quinn."

"You will," Celeste said.

It sounded like a threat, Ginny realized with a sinking heart.

"THE FILE WAS a spreadsheet of the month's payroll." Anson felt chilled to the bone, and it wasn't just the walk he'd taken earlier in the cool night air. He'd spent the ten-minute hike through the woods around the safe house trying to make sense of what he'd learned from the diagnostic scan on the file downloads.

There was a rootkit infection in every link on the spreadsheet Ginny had sent to him in early March. He hadn't yet checked to see if any other files he'd downloaded from her were infected, but he doubted they would be. Once the rootkit dropped on the networked computer, it had probably been set up to allow a virus to propagate throughout the entire system. Whoever wrote the malware would be able to control the whole system, bypassing password protections and recording keystrokes.

Anything private recorded on any computer on the network had to be considered compromised, he explained to his grim-faced boss. "I screwed up," he said finally, meeting Quinn's hard gaze. "I should have figured it out sooner. I shouldn't have delegated the search to Tuck—I should have handled it myself."

"You were on administrative leave. Perhaps by design."

"You think Ginny set me up?"

"Ginny or whoever she's working for."

Anson shook his head. "I can't believe it. I saw the extra coding myself, and the file it was in, but—"

Quinn's expression softened. "People can surprise you."

His boss's uncharacteristic sympathy scraped against Anson's raw nerves. "I'm not an idiot. I know that people surprise you. They do it all the time. But—"

"But Ginny Coltrane is different?"

When Quinn said the words, they sounded foolish. But Ginny *was* different. Anson felt it, bone deep, even if he couldn't explain his instincts to his skeptical boss.

Ginny *had* surprised him over the past couple of days, more than once, but the surprises had all been good ones. She was stronger, braver, smarter and more resourceful than he'd imagined, and while he could understand Quinn's reaction to the apparent evidence of her treachery, he didn't buy it.

Something wasn't right. There was a piece of the story missing, and he had to figure out what it was before Ginny got railroaded by Quinn's investigation.

"Tonight, when you went outside to check on Murdock when you saw the security booth empty, how long were you gone from the building?"

He tried to remember. "Half an hour at least."

"When did Ginny show up?"

"Around the time I decided to give up the search outside and get in contact with you." He narrowed his eyes, starting to see where Quinn was going with this line of questioning. "You can't think Ginny was the one who took my computer. What would she have done with it?"

"She was alone in the building for nearly thirty minutes, Daughtry. Maybe she hid it somewhere."

He shook his head. "She wasn't alone. She told me she thought there was someone else there." He told Quinn what Ginny had told him about the light in the bedroom and the T-shirt that had been moved. "She also heard noises behind her when she was heading upstairs to find me."

"Did you witness any of those events?"

"No, I was outside."

Quinn nodded slowly. "So all you have is Ginny's word, right?"

Damn it. Quinn was right. All he had was Ginny's word. He hadn't heard any of the noises or noticed anything out of place at the office until they'd headed back up to the computer office and found his laptop missing.

"I need to talk to Ginny," he said aloud. "Alone."

Quinn shot him a questioning look. "You're not an interrogator. You have no training in how to question a hostile witness."

"But I know how to talk to Ginny."

Quinn looked up at Jeff Benton, who stood

nearby, quietly observing the conversation. Benton shrugged.

Anson waited until Quinn's gaze returned to him before he spoke. "I've just been through a few months of having my integrity questioned. It stinks. I won't do it to Ginny, not if there's a chance she's innocent."

Quinn's eyes narrowed. "You really think that's a possibility?"

"I have to find out. I know what technical questions to ask. And she seems to trust me." He lowered his voice. "I'll give her an out. See if she takes it. I do know how to ask questions."

"What are you going to do if she confesses?"

"Tell you the truth," he answered.

"And what if she doesn't?"

Anson rose, hearing the sound of concession in his boss's voice. "Then I'm going to find out who's setting her up."

Celeste Kuiper looked up when Anson entered the bedroom. "Quinn said you can leave us alone."

Ginny met his gaze, her eyes wide and scared. He didn't know how to comfort her, or if he even should, so he turned to watch Celeste leave.

"What's going on, Anson?" Ginny caught his arm, tugging him back to face her. Her voice held a shiver of fear that made his stomach hurt. "Has something happened to Danny?"

"No," he assured her quickly. "We don't have any news on your brother."

"Then what is it? Why am I on lockdown?"

"Sit down. We need to talk."

Unease darkened her eyes as she sat on the end of the bed as he directed. He pulled up the desk chair and took her hands in his. Her fingers were icy cold; he warmed them between his hands.

"You're scaring me," she murmured.

"I don't mean to. I just need to know something about the people in your unit."

She blinked. "My unit?"

"At The Gates. Basically, I need to know who does what in Payroll."

The question seemed to catch her off guard. A

nervous laugh escaped her throat. "This is about the Payroll Department? Really?"

"How many people work in Payroll?"

"Four," she answered. "Plus our outside accountant."

"Who does what?"

She released a gusty sigh, starting to relax. "You should know that already, Anson."

"Remind me."

"There's Donna Bailey—she handles timekeeping and coordinates paychecks. Garry Fielding is the benefits coordinator. Jessie Logan handles employee relations and I'm the payroll accountant. I handle most of the paperwork."

"Like tax forms, bookkeeping—"

"Right."

"So when I get those monthly spreadsheets, that's you, too?"

She nodded, her eyes narrowing. "Yes. Why?"

"You put them together yourself? Or do you delegate?"

"I do it myself." She frowned, her gaze sliding

from his face to a point behind him. Her eyes widened. "Oh, my God."

"Ginny—"

She pulled her hands from his. "You were doing a scan on some files or something earlier. When I came in."

"Ginny, it's okay—"

Her gaze snapped back to meet his. "What did you find? Was there an infection like you thought?"

He nodded.

"And it was in one of the spreadsheets I sent you?"

He nodded again.

She shook her head, looking sick. "That's not possible."

"Why?"

"Because I don't know anything about computers other than how to turn them on, change a few minor things and use the more common programs. I swear to you, Anson. I don't."

"Does someone else help you with the files? Maybe someone else in Payroll?"

She shook her head, looking scared and angry at the same time. "I do those files myself. It's part of my job description, and I don't delegate things that are expected of me. I know the importance of getting it right—oh, God. Anson, are you sure?"

He nodded. "I am. There's malicious code in every link in that spreadsheet. When I opened the file and clicked any one of those links, it dropped the rootkit into the system and allowed a specific bit of malware to start propagating throughout the network."

She covered her face with her hands. "That's not possible. It's not."

"And nobody has access to your computer at the office?"

She dropped her hands to her lap. "Well, sure, people have access, but they'd have to know my password, and I've never shared it with anyone."

"Could they have guessed it?"

She shook her head. "I don't think so. It's not a

name or a birthday or anything like that. It's just a number and letter sequence I picked out and memorized. It doesn't correspond to anything."

"Does anyone else know it?"

"No, I told you. I never told anyone my password."

"Not even your brother?"

She stared at him a moment. For the briefest moment, her eyes widened, but she quickly recovered. "No, he doesn't know my password for my work computer."

Oh, hell, Anson thought. There was just enough hesitation in her voice to make his chest tighten with dread. "But he knows the password for your home computer, right?"

She closed her eyes and nodded.

Clues began to click into place, pieces missing but enough of the picture there for him to start putting it all together. "Just four of you in Payroll, and we're adding agents all the time. Plus all that overtime to sort out. And the benefits are worked out contract by contract—it must be crazy trying to keep up with all the details. Especially when you have a brother on disability, a brother with a drinking problem, who's suddenly your responsibility."

Tears welled in her eyes. "Anson, please—"

"It must be hard to keep up with the pace, considering everything you have on you."

She squeezed her eyes shut. Tears spilled down her cheeks. "Stop. Okay. I did it. I took work home. I know I'm not supposed to, but there was just so much to do, and I didn't want anyone to think I couldn't keep up the pace—"

"You worked on the payroll spreadsheet at home?"

She nodded, sniffing. "In February. For the first March payroll. It was so crazy at the office that month, and Danny was having trouble coping with being on disability. He'd go drinking and then call me at work. He was so depressed, and I was worried that he was going to do something destructive—"

Anson's chest tightened with sympathy. "So you had to get things done however you could."

"I took the work home on a flash drive. I didn't think—it's just Danny and me there, and he barely knows how to log in to a computer. So I don't know how—"

"Does he know the password to your computer at home?"

"Yes."

"Could he have accessed the contents of the flash drive at any point?"

She wiped the tears away from her eyes with her fingertips. "I never left the flash drive in my computer. I always put it in my purse when I was done, but—"

"But he could have gotten it out of your purse while you were asleep?" Anson prodded gently, starting to understand just how the rootkit infection could have been embedded in the spreadsheet. If they were right about Danny's connection to the Blue Ridge Infantry, then he'd also have connections to some pretty savvy computer hackers who'd know their way around malware.

"He wouldn't—" She stopped short, her face crumpling. "How could he do it? I swear, he knows less about computers than I do. Unless—"

"Unless he facilitated access for someone else," Anson said, his heart sinking.

Chapter Fourteen

Ginny pressed her face into her hands, feeling sick. "Oh, God."

Anson's voice was gentle. Tinged with pity that made her cringe. "Did he know you were bringing work home?"

She nodded, trying hard to hold back the tears burning her eyes. "He told me I was letting Quinn push me too hard. That I should stand up to him and tell him to hire me an assistant. I couldn't seem to get it through to him that I was lucky to have the job at all and that I had an obligation to do my best work, whatever it took." She lifted her face, but she couldn't quite meet his gaze, feeling a wretched blend of shame and heartbreak at the thought of her brother's possible treachery.

How could Danny have done something like that to her? He knew how damn hard she'd been working to keep a roof over their heads and food on the table. He knew the stress she was under, how many nights she couldn't sleep for worrying about whether or not they'd be able to make the mortgage payment that month.

Was he really so selfish, so damaged, that he'd throw her under the bus that way? What the hell had happened to the brother she'd grown up with, that sweet guy who'd been her biggest champion?

A quiet knock on the door made Ginny jump, her jangling nerves sending tremors through her arms and legs. She looked up at the door, her stomach trembling with anxiety.

Anson put his hand on her knee. "It's okay. I'll get it."

He crossed to the door and opened it a few inches. Quinn was on the other side of the door.

"We heard what she said." Though he spoke in a low tone, Ginny heard every word.

"You were recording us?" Fury and humiliation burned like fire in her belly, propelling her to her feet. She tugged Anson out of the way and faced Quinn through the narrow opening of the doorway. "You honestly believed I was the mole?"

"I had to know what you knew." Quinn's calm, reasonable tone made her want to punch him right in his mouth.

"Then you should have just asked me yourself instead of sending your errand boy in here to soften me up," she snapped, turning her glare on Anson. He stared back at her, his dark gaze dishearteningly opaque.

"He didn't know the room was bugged," Quinn said.

"I don't believe you." She continued staring at Anson, willing him to deny it.

But she knew he couldn't. She saw the truth in those dark eyes.

"You knew," she accused.

"I suspected," he admitted with reluctance. "Quinn was a spy for years. I couldn't see him not using every tool at his disposal to learn what you knew."

"And you didn't warn me."

"I wanted Quinn to hear the truth from you. Because I knew you weren't the person who did this," Anson said flatly, finally meeting her gaze with something other than regret. His eyes flashed with conviction. "You don't have that kind of treachery in you. But I knew Quinn wouldn't take my word for it."

"Am I being legally detained?" She turned to look at Quinn.

"No."

"Then I'd like to get out of here. Now." She pushed past Anson and Quinn and headed down the hall.

"You're not in trouble." Quinn's calm voice halted Ginny in her tracks as she headed toward the front door of the safe house.

She turned to look at him. "I'm not stupid. I know the consequences for breaking protocols."

"You should have come to me and explained your situation, yes. We could have worked something out. Temporary leave, maybe, or called in a temp to help you keep up the pace of the work until the situation normalized. But I believe you when you say you didn't intentionally infect the computer system with a virus."

"You just think my brother did."

"I think your brother is an alcoholic who's gotten mixed up in something very dangerous. He may be under stresses you know nothing about, and he may have done something he wouldn't normally do if he were a well man."

She shook her head. "You don't have to talk to me like I'm an idiot. I know Danny did this. There's no one else who could have done it. But you'll have to excuse me if I'm a little more worried about whether or not he's still alive than whether or not he infected the computers at The Gates."

She kept walking to the door, half expecting Quinn or one of the safe house guards to try to stop her. But nobody intervened, and she made it out of the house without incident.

Outside the air was chilly and damp from the recent rain. Scudding clouds drifted across a waxing moon, but enough light peeked through to reveal a fog-swallowed landscape of trees and underbrush as far as the eye could see.

Anson had told her that Quinn had selected a safe house that wasn't on the company's official list of properties. Unfortunately for Ginny, this unofficial safe house was a large log cabin in the middle of the Smoky Mountains, miles from any well-traveled road. Not that she had a car at her disposal or anyone she could call to pick her up, now that Danny was missing.

And what was she hoping to do, anyway? Where could she go now? She didn't have the resources to find her brother or the know-how to locate him. She didn't even know who his friends were, who he might try to contact if he managed to get away from whoever took him from the hospital.

Tears pricked her eyes. She blinked them away, angry at herself. At Danny. At the whole damned world.

She heard the door to the safe house open and shut behind her. Part of her, the part driven purely by stubborn pride, wanted to start walking and not look back. But the sensible side reminded her that walking out of these hills alone would be neither easy nor safe.

"You sort of hate me, don't you?" Anson's voice was closer than she'd expected. A moment later, she felt a wall of heat at her back as he closed the distance between them.

"I don't hate you," she answered. "I don't particularly like you at the moment, though."

"I guess I deserve that."

"You could have warned me about the bug."

"I could've. But I don't think it would have served your purposes to know about it. You might have sounded nervous instead of truthful."

"So you kept it from me for my own good."

He laid his hand on her shoulder. His touch spread warmth through her body, radiating from the point of contact. "Quinn's not going to fire you."

"I'm resigning."

"Why?" He tugged her shoulder, pulling her around to face him. "You're not the one who did this. Everybody knows that."

"But I did. I broke protocol. I disobeyed the rules. Maybe I wasn't the one who created the malware, but it was my fault it got into the system." And people had nearly died because of it, she realized with a flood of guilt. A shiver rippled through her and didn't stop.

"It's been detected now. And we know where it came from, so we can try to trace it back to the person who created it."

"How? We don't where Danny is. We don't even know if he's alive."

He wrapped his arms around her shaking body and pulled her tightly to him. "Quinn will find him. And Danny can tell us how that malware made it onto your flash drive."

"He doesn't know enough about computers to have done it." She looked up at Anson. "Clearly there's a lot I don't know about my brother these days, but I'm certain of that much."

"But there are hackers working with the BRI who could have done it. In fact, it's pretty much what they live to do." He let her go as she pulled away and turned her back to him again. "Your brother knew you were bringing work home, didn't he?"

"Yes, of course. I couldn't exactly spend half my night chained to my computer without his knowing it." Her shoulders slumped with despair. "He knew how important it was for me to keep my job."

Anson didn't say anything, but she could feel his anger. The only thing he knew about Danny was what he'd witnessed over the past few days, and her brother hadn't exactly covered himself with glory. But there was another side of Danny.

A sweet side. A kind side. When he was sober, he was funny and good-hearted. He'd do anything she asked of him, just because he loved her and wanted her to be happy.

She couldn't forget that Danny just because he had a drinking problem.

"I know you don't understand why I want to protect him."

"I do understand," Anson said quietly. "I just don't think trying to protect him is going to be good for either of you in the end."

"Because it wasn't good for you and your father?" She turned to look at him, anger burning in her chest. "Danny's nothing like your father, if anything you've hinted about him is true."

"I'm sure you're right."

"I *am* right."

He caught her hands in his, holding on tightly when she started to tug them away from his grasp. "Ginny, I am not your enemy."

"You want me to turn on Danny."

"I never said that. Not once."

"Then what? What am I supposed to do?" To her dismay, hot tears welled in her eyes and spilled down her cheeks before she could pull her hands away from his grasp.

He let go of her hands, and she wiped the tears away with her fingertips, sniffing back the next flood of tears threatening to spill. She didn't want to look weak in front of Anson. Or anyone else from The Gates. She'd already shown them she couldn't keep up with the workload; the last thing she needed to do was come across as a big cry-baby, as well.

"If you need to cry, go ahead. Nobody's watching."

"*You* are." Her words came out low and tight with anger, revealing more of her inner turmoil than she'd intended.

"I'm not gonna judge you."

She lifted her chin. "Aren't you? It's my fault you've been sitting at home on suspension for the past month."

"We don't know that for sure."

"Don't we? Thanks to those infected links in a spreadsheet I put together, the whole system at The Gates was compromised. God only knows how many secrets were revealed, above and beyond the one that led to your suspension. And Nick Darcy's, too." She felt sick at the thought. "I don't know how you or anyone else at The Gates can bear to look at me."

Anson cupped her cheeks between his palms, making her look at him. "Because *you* didn't do it, Ginny. Danny took advantage of your conscientiousness. He betrayed your trust."

She pushed his hands away. "No, damn it! You don't get to talk about him that way."

Anson released a long, frustrated sigh. "Do you want me to go away?"

Part of her did. Part of her wanted him to go away and stay away, and then maybe she could pretend that everything she'd been through, everything she'd learned about her brother's problems, was all a lie.

But if life with her mercurial mother had taught

her anything, it was the folly of living in a dream world. Reality never went away, and the sooner you faced your problems, the sooner you could find a way past them.

It was just—how was she supposed to get past this problem? Danny had almost certainly colluded with someone to open a back door into The Gates' computer system—and all the sensitive material it contained. God knew how many cases had been compromised by her mistake.

But far worse, Danny was missing. And he might not even be alive.

"Don't shut me out, Ginny. Let me help you."

"How?" Once again, hot tears stung her eyes. She blinked hard, trying to keep them back, afraid that once she started crying, she'd never be able to stop again. "There's nothing anyone can do until we can find Danny. And I don't even know where to start looking."

"I think I do." Anson reached out and thumbed away a tear that had spilled from her eye. "Come on, let's go back inside. We'll figure out something, I promise."

She wanted to believe he was right. That there was an answer and they still had time to find it.

But she was terrified it was already too late.

ALEXANDER QUINN TURNED away from the window facing out on the moonlit front yard of the safe house and answered his trilling cell phone. "Marbury Motors twenty-four-hour hotline."

"My engine is knocking," a female voice drawled in his hear.

"Then answer it," he replied with a smile.

"Just heard from Sara Lindsey," Olivia Sharp said on a sigh. "The hospital security camera malfunctioned. No video available during the time that Danny Coltrane went missing."

Quinn grimaced. "What are the odds?"

"Not great. Deputy Lindsey thinks there was probably some inside help disabling the security video so we wouldn't be able to identify the assailant."

"If he was an assailant." Quinn looked up as the front door opened and Ginny entered, Anson right behind her. Ginny didn't meet his eyes as she walked through the kitchen toward the back of the house, but Anson's gaze locked with his for a moment, communicating an unspoken warning. *She's off-limits.*

He needed to work on his management skills. Too damn many of his agents were getting too big for their britches, as his mama would have said.

"Deputy Lindsey did say they'd found a few witnesses who thought they could pick out the man with Danny Coltrane from a lineup. They're meeting with a sketch artist right now. She's hoping she'll have a sketch of the suspect soon. She promised to let us know."

One benefit of some of his agents getting romantically involved with the local police, he supposed—Sara Lindsey wasn't going to play power games with the agents from The Gates just because she wore a uniform and a badge. Thanks to her relationship with Cain Dennison, she knew that they were on the same side, at least in this particular case. She'd accept their help and share what information she could.

"So I got an alert not to use the company computer or anything connected to the server."

"The entire system has been compromised."

"Lovely."

"Daughtry's on it."

"So he's back in the fold?" She sounded surprised.

"You have a problem with that?"

"No. The agent I had assigned to him insists he's squeaky clean."

Quinn smiled. "You never call him by name."

"You told me to be discreet."

"Yes, but I already know who it is."

"Fine. Marty Tucker swears he's squeaky-clean." Olivia sighed. "I guess if the system is compromised somehow, that explains how all the information about your former employee got into the wrong hands."

"But the question is still who has been controlling the network?"

"What does Daughtry say?"

"He isn't sure. But we still have reason to believe it was someone who works at The Gates," he pointed out, thinking about the break-in at the office earlier that evening. "Whoever got inside was there before Anson opened the door and went outside, if we're to believe Ginny Coltrane."

"And are we to believe Ginny Coltrane?" Olivia asked, sounding skeptical.

Quinn thought about what he knew of Ginny, what he'd heard through the listening device Celeste Kuiper had planted in Anson's bedroom. She'd sounded confused, horrified and ultimately ashamed. Maybe Quinn's instincts were wrong and it was all an act to cover her tracks.

But his gut was telling him Ginny was telling the truth. And he'd made it through twenty years of covert operations by trusting his gut.

"We are to believe Ginny Coltrane," he said decisively. "So that means there was someone in the building with her and Daughtry tonight. And the only way in was by using a code that even Daughtry didn't have access to."

"Could Danny Coltrane have the code?"

"I don't think so. I'll find out, though."

"Assuming he didn't, could the hacker who infected the computer system have gotten the code from an email alert about the door code change?" Olivia asked.

"I didn't send it out by email. Too insecure. I called every agent into my office and gave them the code personally, just as I gave it to you."

She sighed. "So I have to start over from scratch?"

"I'll get back to you on that." He hung up and headed down the hall to the bedrooms. Daughtry's door was open, so Quinn walked in and found his IT director sitting in front of the computer array, his elbows on the desk and his hands folded under his chin. Ginny was sitting on his bed, her legs crossed and her head slumped.

"Just the person I needed to talk to," Quinn said, making them both jump.

"Which one of us?" Daughtry asked, rising from the desk chair and moving to stand between Quinn and Ginny. If it weren't so annoying, Quinn might have been amused by his IT director's sudden protective tendencies.

"Ginny, although you may stay." He sidestepped Daughtry and crossed to where Ginny sat looking at him with baleful blue eyes. "Was there any possible way your brother could have gained access to the door code at The Gates? Did you write the code anywhere he might have seen it?"

She shook her head. "I didn't write it down. I memorized it immediately."

"Did you ever use the code where Danny could have seen the keypad on the front lock?"

"No. I don't know that he's ever stepped foot on the property, but he certainly hasn't been there with me."

"Okay, thank you."

As he started to leave, Daughtry caught his arm. "It's an inside job, isn't it? Someone had to have the code to get into the office tonight."

"Yes." He met Daughtry's eyes. "Which means we still have a mole at The Gates."

Chapter Fifteen

Anson managed a couple of hours of sleep before morning sunlight angled through the curtains of the safe-house bedroom and slanted across his face. With a grumble, he rolled over and bumped into a solid form on the bed beside him.

"Ow." Ginny's voice was thick with sleep, and she gave him a little nudge back to his side of the bed.

Blinking away the remnants of sleep, he turned his head to look at her, trying to remember how they'd managed to get in the same bed. She'd left his room before he went to bed, hadn't she?

Was this even his room?

A quick look around convinced him he hadn't

sleepwalked to Ginny's room sometime in the night. Which meant—

"I guess you're wondering what I'm doing here." She pushed herself up to her elbows and looked at him through a mess of sleep-tousled hair.

"The question had crossed my mind."

"I got spooked in the other bedroom. Kept hearing noises outside the window." Embarrassment pinked her cheeks. "I know it was probably just the wind or maybe raccoons out foraging, but all I could remember was how creeped out I was last night at the office, when I realized my things weren't the way I'd left them. Then I couldn't remember if the chair in my bedroom had been sitting so close to the bed when I went to sleep, which *really* creeped me out."

"So you came in here?"

"I was hoping you were still awake, but you'd already sacked out."

"So you just crawled into bed with me?" He waggled his eyebrows at her, hiding a smile as she turned a deeper shade of pink, and waved his hand at his disheveled appearance. He hadn't even made it under the blankets, and he was still in the jeans and T-shirt he'd changed into before Quinn had sent them packing to the safe house. At least he'd thought to take off his shoes, though he was still wearing his socks. "Who could blame you? It takes a strong woman to resist my outrageous sexual charms."

She grinned at him, some of her nervousness abating. "And yet, somehow I managed."

He clapped his hand over his heart, feigning injury. "Ow."

She pushed up to a sitting position, revealing that she'd slept in her clothes, as well. Of course, the way that T-shirt was pulling tight over her breasts and her jeans were hugging her curvy hips, he didn't think her fully clothed state would have been much of a deterrent to his libido had he known she was going to crawl into his bed and stay awhile.

It wasn't doing much to quell it now.

"You're not mad, are you?" she asked.

"At finding a pretty woman in my bed? Never."

She blushed again, and he felt an answering heat rising into his neck and cheeks, though for his part, embarrassment had nothing to do with it.

But as he started to lean closer, drawn by her soft, sleepy heat, her next words hit him like a dash of cold water. "I'm going to tell Quinn I'm going home today."

He sat up quickly to face her. "What? Are you crazy?"

"I've been thinking about it. A lot. I don't think either of us is in any immediate danger. Last night at The Gates, I was in the shower and vulnerable when the intruder was down there. If he wanted to hurt me, he could've easily made it happen. But he just wanted to scare me away."

"He coldcocked Dale Murdock. Gave him a concussion." Fortunately, it looked like Murdock was going to be okay. Before Quinn left for the night, he'd received a call from the hospital reassuring him that Dale Murdock's injuries didn't seem to be life-threatening. But he was going to be staying in the hospital overnight for observation.

"But that was so he could get into the building without being stopped. He didn't try to hurt you, either, did he?"

"No," he admitted. "Just stole my computer."

"That was to cover his tracks. Or try, anyway." She nodded toward the computer setup on the desk at the foot of the bed. "Any luck finding out how much of the system has been compromised?"

"We have to assume everything has," he said with a grimace, swinging his legs over the side of the bed. He needed a trip to the bathroom and coffee, in that order. Maybe a shower somewhere in there.

"So what are you going to do now?" She stood up as well, meeting him at the door and looking up at him with a heady mixture of admiration and confidence, as if she was certain he could handle whatever trouble he found in the computer system at The Gates.

He didn't know whether to feel flattered or terrified. "I need to clean out the rootkit infection, for starters. But I want to be careful, because I also want to see if I can figure out who's been pulling the strings behind the scenes. Whoever took control of the network was working inside The Gates. I think that much is fairly obvious."

"How many people at The Gates are capable of doing such a thing?"

"Once the rootkit infects the system, I'm not sure the person doing the controlling would need a high level of computer know-how. All they'd need to do is follow someone else's instructions. There might be things that they could do from within The Gates that an outside person might not be able to accomplish." He needed to give that idea a little more thought.

"I want to go home, Anson. I want to clean up the mess in my house and start focusing on trying to find Danny." She pushed her messy hair back from her face, revealing her crinkled brow and the worry lines around her blue eyes. "There might be something in his things that could lead us to who he's with."

"Don't you think the sheriff's department has already thought of that? Or for that matter, Quinn's investigators? You should let them do their jobs and concentrate on keeping yourself safe."

"How can you ask that of me? If it was your brother out there somewhere, with a stab wound in his side and God knows who holding him prisoner, could you just sit around all day and do nothing?"

He felt her frustration keenly, felt an answering burn in his gut that answered her question. "No, I couldn't."

"I've got to have something constructive to do, Anson, or I'm going to go crazy." She closed the distance between them, curling her fingers in the front of his T-shirt. "Get me out of here. Let's just go drive around a little. I know some of the places Danny frequented. Maybe we can ask people some questions, see if they might know who he's been hanging around with over the past few months."

She smelled good. Soft and sweet like a summer morning. He felt the disconcerting urge to bury his face in her hair and never move again.

"I'll have to clear it with Quinn," he said finally.

She frowned. "He'll say no. You know he will."

"You think the guards will let us go without his permission?"

She made a face. "We're not prisoners, are we? We'll just tell them we're going. What are they going to do, detain us?"

She was in a rebellious mood this morning, and it was sparking his own pugnacious streak. Why shouldn't they leave if they wanted to? He thought she was probably right about the intruder at The Gates the night before. While the intruder had put Murdock out of commission in order to get into the office undetected, he hadn't bothered

Anson or Ginny, though he'd had the chance to do so. He'd simply waited for his chance to grab the laptop, then left without incident.

"Are you sure you want to go home?" he asked. "We could go to my place instead. It's right on a main street in town, surrounded by businesses and lots of people."

"But Danny's things are at the house." Her fingers playing against his chest, she edged closer, slanting a look up at him through lowered lashes. "I want to go through everything myself. There might be things the police didn't find or didn't know were significant."

Anson looked down at her, warning bells going off in his head suddenly. Since when was Ginny Coltrane a flirt?

Since she wanted to leave the safe house, he realized.

"What do you think?" She looked up at him with a hopeful expression, but he saw a hint of desperation behind those soft blue eyes.

Something was definitely up.

But what?

There was only one way to find out, he realized, his gut tightening at the thought. He had to get her out of here and see what happened next— then hope like hell he was up to handling it.

"Let's get out of here," he said, pasting on a smile.

SHE HATED LYING. Hated deception of any sort, really. Thanks to her mother's reckless choices, she'd seen the mess lies could make in a person's life, ripping away the ability to trust, piece by piece, until there was nothing left but hard-eyed resignation to a life of constant disappointment.

But the text she'd received shortly before daybreak had left her with few choices.

Anson was her only way out of the safe house. She knew that much. Quinn might have told her she was free to leave, but she was pretty sure he'd given the guards orders not to let her leave alone.

But as she'd hoped, they didn't stop them when Anson said they needed to get out and take care of a few things in town they hadn't had a chance to deal with before they were spirited away to the safe house.

Fortunately, they'd let Anson bring his car with him the night before. They were on the road as soon as they'd eaten a quick breakfast.

"We'll go to your place first," he said once they were back on the main highway. "Then to my place to pick up a few things, okay? Then we go back to the safe house."

"We could split up and be finished even faster," she suggested, trying to make the suggestion sound casual. "I got a text this morning from the auto shop in Purgatory. My car is ready. You could take me to pick it up and then I could drive to the house while you grab some stuff from the loft—"

"I thought the idea was to stick together," Anson protested, slanting a curious look her way.

"And to fly under Quinn's radar," she added in what she hoped was a reasonable tone. "We'd be through with our errands in no time and back to the safe house before Quinn even realizes we were gone."

"You'd be alone at your house for at least an hour."

"I lived there alone for a couple of years before Danny moved back in," she said with a sigh. "Those bastards have Danny. Why would they come after me? I don't know anything about what he was into, and they have to know it."

"I suppose you're right," Anson said slowly.

"I could even pack up anything of Danny's that the sheriff's department didn't confiscate, and we could go through it together back at the safe house."

Anson smiled at that suggestion. "Now you're just tempting me. You know I long to play Hardy Boys to your Nancy Drew."

"I was always more a Trixie Belden girl," she said with a bright grin, feeling the tide turning in her direction. "Drop me off at the garage and then go on to your loft. I'll run home, grab as much stuff as I can and meet you at the loft. I can be done in under an hour."

"I don't mind hanging with you while you go through things."

"I know you don't." She tried not to let her frustration show. Anson didn't deserve to be treated like a nuisance. He was anything but, and if the text message she'd found on her phone that morning had been the least bit ambiguous, she would have told him all about it.

But the directions had been starkly clear:

If u want to see ur brother alive again, be @ Black Creek Dam, noon. Women's bathroom, stall 2, 4 ur next instructions. Come alone. We're watching.

"It'll take me fifteen minutes to get what I need at the loft. I'll be at your place in twenty minutes, tops," Anson said finally. "Sound like a deal?"

She nearly wilted with relief. "Sounds perfect. Just drop me off at the car place. That'll give you a head start and maybe you can get to my place in time to help me go through some of Danny's things."

"Okay." Anson slanted a quick look at her before he had to turn his attention back to the twisty mountain road.

Ginny looked down at her hands, hating herself for lying but knowing she hadn't had any other options. Maybe she should have told Anson the truth, shown him the text message and gotten the whole crew at The Gates in on the action.

But whoever had Danny had managed to spirit him out of the hospital despite the security staff there being on high alert. And the same person or people could have been behind the break-in at The Gates.

We're watching, the text message had warned.

She knew they almost certainly were.

WHEN ANSON DROVE away from McLemore's Garage, he went only half a block before parking his car and waiting for Ginny Coltrane to make her move.

She was a bad liar. She'd tried hard to be nonchalant about it, but her fear and desperation had bled through her sunny facade, convincing him his initial impression was the correct one: she was up to something, and it wasn't something he'd like.

Five minutes later, Ginny drove to the car shop's exit, shiny new tires in the place of the ones that had been slashed at the Whiskey Road Tavern, and made a right turn out of the lot.

Away from her house in Two Souls Hollow.

He pulled out and followed, taking care to keep several car lengths between them.

One of the benefits of working at The Gates was access to training personnel skilled in functioning efficiently in high-risk environments. While the support staff wasn't required to take more than a basic self-defense and risk-assessment course, Quinn had made all training courses available to employees who wanted to improve their threat-management skills.

Anson had taken advantage of the opportunities, mostly to test his own mettle. His hardscrabble early life had left him with a lot of internal scars, but outwardly, it had hardened him. The only way to stay ahead of his father's drunken outbursts was to be faster and tougher than the old man. By the time he graduated high school, he was half a foot taller than his father and outweighed him by thirty pounds, most of it muscle.

But his more cerebral pursuits during college and afterward had left him softer. Slower. As much as he'd hated a life lived on the edge of a drunk's anger, he'd also found himself missing the adrenaline rush of staying one step ahead of the old man, as well.

When Quinn's headhunters had found him working for a software company in Knoxville, it hadn't been the job description that had lured him away to The Gates. It had been the prospect of once again functioning in a high-risk environment.

"Well, now you have what you were looking for, Daughtry," he muttered as he took the turn onto Black Creek Parkway, keeping pace with Ginny's little Ford about sixty yards ahead. "Congratulations."

His cell phone rang as he spotted Ginny taking a turn off the parkway onto the narrow two-lane road that led south toward Black Creek Dam. He glanced up at the dashboard phone holder and saw the number was blocked on the phone display. After two more rings, he took a chance and hit the speaker button. "Daughtry."

"Where the hell did you take Ginny Coltrane?" Alexander Quinn didn't hide his anger.

Anson sighed. He should have known there was no such thing as flying under Alexander Quinn's radar.

For a second, he considered making something up. But Quinn also had a built-in lie detector in his brain, and Anson wasn't much better at lying than Ginny was.

"I'm not sure," he replied, trying to keep far enough back that Ginny wouldn't spot him. But on the lightly traveled two-lane, with no cars between them, it wasn't easy being inconspicuous.

He had to hope she was too focused on her destination to pay much attention to any vehicles in her rearview mirror.

"I suggest you become sure in the next ten seconds," Quinn barked.

"She came to me this morning pretending to be suffering from cabin fever." Anson had to speed up to be certain he didn't lose sight of Ginny's car around the sharp bend ahead. "But I could tell she was up to something."

"Up to what?"

"She talked me into getting her out of the safe house. The plan was for us to go to her place in Two Souls Hollow and see if the sheriff's department could have missed any clues among Danny's things. Then we were going to go to my place to pick up a few more things for me and return to the safe house. Should have taken no more than an hour or two."

"But the plan changed?" Quinn surmised, still sounding pissed.

"Once we were in the car, she told me she'd gotten a text that the repairs on her car were finished and she could pick it up from McLemore's. She put a whole lot of effort into convincing me that we needed to split up—she'd go to the house, I'd go to my place and we'd meet up when she was done. It would cut our time away from the safe house in half."

"And I might not even know you were gone?"

"Something like that."

Quinn muttered a low curse. "Where is she now?"

"About fifty yards ahead of me on Deception Lake Road." Ginny's taillights flashed red as she started to slow down ahead. They were getting close to the dam, he realized.

Why was she going to Black Creek Dam?

"Could you be more specific?" Quinn asked.

"We're about a quarter mile from Black Creek Dam." As he watched, Ginny took the turn into the small parking lot next to the dam that created the southern end of Deception Lake. At this point, *creek* was a misnomer; Black Creek was as much a river as the Ketoowee River that flowed into Deception Lake to the north. Just below the dam, the frequently released flow of water through turbines attracted game fish, making the area a prime fishing spot.

But Anson was pretty sure Ginny hadn't come to Black Creek Dam to go fishing. Not for bluegills, anyway.

"She just parked near the public restrooms," he told Quinn as Ginny exited her car and looked around nervously. "Maybe she just had to take a pit stop."

"On her way to where?"

Excellent question, Anson thought. "I'm going to see if I can get closer."

"Do that. Meanwhile, I'm going to get you some backup."

"You think I need backup?"

"You're not an agent."

Anson pulled his car into a parking place at the far end of the parking lot and settled in to see what Ginny did next. "And she's not a criminal."

"But she's obviously doing something underhanded, wouldn't you agree?" Quinn asked.

"Define *underhanded*," Anson murmured as Ginny walked around the small restroom pavilion, disappearing from sight. He sat forward, wishing the parking lot had a view of the restroom entrances. But all he could see was the windowless brick wall at the back of the pavilion. He didn't like losing sight of her that way, especially since the pavilion blocked a large part of his view of the grassy walkway between the parking lot and the dam itself.

"She lied to you. Wouldn't you say that's underhanded?"

"Maybe she had a reason." Anson could think of at least one possible reason—maybe her brother had managed to get in touch.

Was he waiting for her?

A sudden rush of movement on the other side of

the pavilion caught Anson's attention. A cream-colored panel van rolled up next to the restroom pavilion, the side door sliding open just as a man dressed in camouflage from head to toe came running out from behind the pavilion, dragging a struggling Ginny Coltrane with him.

Anson jerked the car door open and started running, but the panel van door slammed and the vehicle was off before he got within thirty yards.

He ran back to his car, his heart racing as he slid behind the wheel and started the engine. Quinn's voice rose over the cell-phone speaker.

"What the hell just happened?" he barked.

"Someone just grabbed Ginny," Anson replied, gunning the engine as he peeled out of the parking lot in pursuit. "And I'm going to get her back."

Chapter Sixteen

Stupid, stupid, stupid!

Ginny tugged against the plastic restraints anchoring her to a canvas strap attached to the wall of the van, cursing herself for being such a damn fool. She hadn't even let herself think she was walking into a trap. What kind of idiot didn't take that possibility into consideration?

But why would these people want her if they already had Danny? Whatever her brother was into, she knew nothing about it. Surely Danny would have told them that much already?

Or had he been so desperate to take the pressure off himself that he'd lied and made her a target instead?

The fact that she could believe such a thing of her brother made her want to roll up into a ball and cry, but she couldn't give in to self-pity. Not at the moment, tied up and on the road to God only knew where.

She'd gotten only a brief glimpse of her captor before he'd shoved her into the waiting van. Six feet tall, a little on the burly side, with an unkempt brown beard and hard brown eyes visible beneath the brim of his woods-pattern camouflage cap.

The men in the van had been similarly dressed, though one had been fair-skinned and sandy-haired, and the other older, with more gray in his beard and the shaggy hair peeking out from beneath his cap.

She knew she'd seen the sandy-haired man once before, she realized before the man jammed a pillowcase over her head, blocking out half of the daylight and all of her view of the van's occupants.

Then the van door had slammed and they'd

accelerated quickly, nearly pitching her headfirst into the floorboard. Only the restraining hands of her captors kept her upright.

They hadn't let her go until they'd latched her to the canvas strap attached to the inside wall of the van. Now she clung to the strap to keep from sliding around as the van barreled forward to whatever their destination might be.

They were headed into the mountains. That much she could tell by the shifts in the van's momentum, caused no doubt by the sharp curves and twisting switchbacks as they circled their way up the peaks. Was that where they had Danny?

Or was Danny even alive anymore?

Don't think that way. Keep your head. Remember what you learned at The Gates.

Most of what she'd learned was self-defense, but even those lessons had gone out the window when the man who'd grabbed her outside the restroom first slammed her face into the brick wall, stunning her just long enough for him to take control and hustle her out to the van. Even now, the injured side of her face was aching like hell, and she was pretty sure that warm, wet sensation trickling down her cheeks was blood, not tears, if the metallic smell was anything to go by.

But now she had time to think. To assess. To recall the things she'd learned during her training period at The Gates.

Adam Brand, a former FBI agent with years of experience, had been her instructor, and one of the things he'd taught the whole group was how to survive a kidnapping. *It's not likely it'll ever happen to you,* he'd told them with a laugh, *but just working in an environment like The Gates increases your risk somewhat. Better safe than sorry. And it's a good exercise in critical thinking, right?*

Right, she thought. Critical thinking. As if her adrenaline-saturated brain cells could handle such a rigorous task.

But that was the point of learning the rules, right? So that she didn't have to think. She could just follow directions.

First rule—try to evade the kidnapping. Too late for that. Move on to the second rule: calm down. Yeah, right.

On to rule three: assess your situation.

She couldn't see anything through the pillow-case, but her ears still worked. So did her other senses. So she concentrated on what she could hear, smell and feel.

The van engine was loud and she could make out a distinct rattle that suggested it wasn't a newer model. She tried to remember what little she'd seen of the vehicle when she'd been trundled through the open door. It had been white, hadn't it? Or off-white, though she couldn't be sure that wasn't a result of several layers of road grime. But overall, her impression had been a boxy white van. Older model—maybe a Ford?

Okay, so she was in an older-model white van, maybe a Ford, with a rattle in the engine. Great. Very helpful—if she managed to make it out alive.

None of her captors was speaking, but she could

hear the soft rush of their breathing. In and out, quicker than normal, suggesting she wasn't the only one experiencing an adrenaline rush. She wasn't sure whether they were scared, as she was, or excited by the prospect of taking her wherever they were going, but either way, she couldn't let herself think about what might lie in store for her at the end of the line.

That way lay madness.

But it did lead her straight to rule number four—figuring out why she'd been kidnapped.

They'd lured her to the dam by invoking her brother's name. Which meant they knew about Danny's disappearance. Most likely, they were the ones who had him, right?

But if they had Danny, and they knew anything about him, surely they realized they could ply him with liquor and get just about anything out of him they wanted to know.

Why did they need her?

Unless…

What if they weren't the people who had Danny, after all?

She thought about the men she'd seen before the pillowcase dropped over her head. Bearded, dressed in camo, with shaggy hair and hard eyes—including one she recognized from the encounter at the parking lot at the Whiskey Road Tavern. Those men had stabbed Danny. They hadn't seemed remotely interested in taking him alive, had they?

So why would they have changed tactics and spirited him out of the hospital alive? And hadn't the witnesses suggested Danny went along with his captor willingly?

She closed her eyes, trying to think. Maybe these people weren't the ones who'd taken him from the hospital. Maybe they had a completely different agenda.

Maybe they were hoping to use her to lure Danny out.

She grabbed the canvas handle bolted to the

side of the van as the vehicle swerved hard into another sharp curve.

"Who are you?" she asked aloud, wondering if anyone would answer.

Nobody did.

KEEPING UP WITH the van wasn't that difficult, but trying to stay undetected while not letting the vehicle out of his sight was pushing Anson's driving skills to the limit. The van had quickly turned off Deception Lake Road onto Woodegaska Road, a twisting two-lane that rose to the top of Broderick Mountain east of the lake.

"That's largely undeveloped," Quinn warned when Anson apprised him of the new direction, his voice tense. On the other end of the line, he heard the noise of a car engine. Quinn was joining the chase. "It's not going to be easy to stay out of sight."

"About that backup you mentioned—" Anson grimaced as he sped a little too quickly into a curve and had to finesse the car back onto the road as it veered terrifyingly close to a steep drop-off.

"On its way. I should have agents blocking every exit from the mountain within ten minutes. Still have them in sight?"

"Barely," he answered as the van disappeared around another twisting curve. He caught up and saw the van's brake lights glow bright red as the vehicle began to slow. "Looks like they're turning off the main road."

Quinn was quiet a moment, then said, "I think they're heading up to the old sawmill near the top of Fowler Rise."

"And you know that because?"

"Because I had Bennett put a GPS tracker on your car while you were asleep," Quinn answered.

"I thought you'd decided not to track us against our will anymore."

"Desperate times..."

Anson sighed. "How much farther does this road go?"

"It ends at the sawmill about a half mile up the road. There's nowhere else for them to go on that road. No other way out except on foot."

Instead of taking the turnoff, Anson drove ahead and parked his car off the road. He was taking a risk, choosing to continue on foot instead of in his car, he knew, but it was also a far more stealthy approach if he wanted to get close enough to make a move to help Ginny if the opportunity arose.

They'd hear his car coming. But on foot, if he was careful, they'd never hear him until he was in position to do some good.

"I have to go radio silent," he told Quinn.

"What are you doing?" his boss asked.

He tugged the phone from the dashboard holder and answered, "I'm heading up to the sawmill on foot."

Then he turned off the phone and shoved it into his pocket as he headed into the woods.

OLIVIA SHARP CROSSED the bull pen of the Ridge County Sheriff's Department, her gaze focused on the dark-haired woman sitting at the desk closest to the windows. Sara Lindsey was at her computer, typing rapidly, her brow furrowed with concentration.

"Careful, Deputy. You'll wear out that keyboard."

Sara leaned back in her desk chair and looked up at Olivia, her eyes narrowing. "Come to check up on the local yokels?"

Olivia grimaced as she pulled up a chair and sat across from the deputy. They still weren't quite at eye level with each other; at nearly six feet tall, Olivia had long since got used to towering over most women and half the men of her acquaintance. But Sara Lindsey didn't strike her as the kind of woman who'd be easily intimidated by someone else's size anyway.

"I was hoping you'd have the composite sketch," Olivia answered, determined not to let the other woman's defensiveness spark her own combative streak. They were, after all, on the same side. In this investigation, at least.

Sara released a long sigh. "Not yet. But does

this description ring any bells?" She pushed a piece of paper across the desk to Olivia.

Olivia picked up the paper. It was a handwritten set of notes, apparently taken from a witness interview. The witness described a clean-shaven male, five-ten or five-eleven, slender build, age twenty-five to thirty-five, with short, sandy hair and brown eyes.

"Not quite the description I was expecting," Sara murmured.

Not what Olivia had been expecting, either. "Definitely not someone with the Blue Ridge Infantry, unless it's a brand-new recruit." The quasi militia favored eschewing razors and regular haircuts, preferring the "living off the land" look, even if their sustenance came from drugs and graft rather than hard, honest work. It fed the illusion that they were like the other tough-minded, independent souls here in the mountains who lived close to the land and nature.

But it was an illusion. They weren't patriots. They certainly weren't honest men making an honest living and trying to keep the government boot off their necks.

They were criminals, thieves, drug dealers and murderers. And they'd killed two of the finest men she'd ever known—and managed to destroy the career of another man who'd never been able to get over what had happened that day over a year ago in Richmond, Virginia, when a BRI member had blown himself up in a warehouse and taken two FBI agents and a handful of civilians with him.

"Know what this sounds like to me?" Sara asked.

"Like one of those pasty-faced trust-fund babies who fancy themselves anarchists?" Olivia answered, letting her Alabama drawl come out to play. Down here in the hills, the rural twang of her Sand Mountain upbringing wasn't the detriment it had been when she was trying to pull herself up the FBI ladder.

Sara smiled at her response. "Exactly like one

of those. We know the anarchists are in league with the BRI."

"We know they *were*," Olivia corrected, drawing a curious look from the deputy. "We think their coalition may be fracturing. At least, we think the BRI has decided to get into the drug trade themselves instead of depending on the cooks and growers here in the hills."

Sara's eyes narrowed. "Taking out the middleman?"

"Exactly."

"But the anarchists weren't that big a part of the drug trade, were they?"

"Only tangentially," Olivia answered. "But as little regard as you or I might have for them and their antisocial posturing, they're not stupid. They have to know that if the BRI is willing to cut out the drug boys, they'll be looking for a way to shuck off the hackers, too."

"So maybe the hackers have decided to fight fire with fire—get into the drug trade themselves. Set themselves up as an alternative to the BRI. Which leads me to the million-dollar question—"

"Which side is Danny Coltrane on?" Olivia finished for her.

Sara nodded as her phone rang. She grabbed it. "Lindsey." She listened for a moment then smiled. "Meet you now."

"What's up?" Olivia asked as Sara rose from her chair.

"Sketch artist is done. He's waiting in interview-room one. Want to come take a look?"

"You bet." Olivia followed Sara through the deputy bull pen and down a short corridor to the first interview room. Inside, a heavyset man in his fifties with a neatly trimmed beard and sparkling blue eyes looked up at their entrance. "The witnesses all agreed this is pretty close," he told Sara, handing over the sketch.

Olivia looked over Sara's shoulder and stared at the all-too-familiar face in the sketch. "I'll be damned."

Sara met her gaze. "I think you just found your mole."

"I DON'T KNOW what you want. Tell me what you want and maybe I can help you."

Only silence greeted Ginny's muffled overture. She was still restrained, her wrists bound in front of her and linked through what felt like a large eyebolt screwed into a cinder-block wall. With time and effort, she might be able to loosen the bolt from the concrete block. Effort she could handle.

Time was the question.

The pillowcase remained over her head, making her feel breathless and claustrophobic. But she knew enough air was coming through the cotton weave as well as under the loose-hanging hem that bunched over her breasts. With her hands bound, she couldn't move the makeshift hood from her head, but she wasn't in danger of suffocating. The smothering sensation was from the fiery panic rising in her throat like bile, threatening to overwhelm her if she didn't find a way to calm herself down.

She was alive. The scraped and bruised places

on the side of her face hurt like hell, but they weren't going to kill her. She hadn't been shot, stabbed or otherwise incapacitated. The kidnappers had taken some care to hide their identities from her by covering her with the hood, which meant they didn't currently have any intentions of killing her.

But that could always change. Wasn't that one of the things Adam Brand had warned about in the risk-management training course?

Things could always change, and the people who survived were those who read the warning signs correctly and knew when and how to make an escape.

She sat very still and silent for a moment, listening. The room wasn't entirely quiet, of course—the building was rustic and drafty, wind whistling through openings in her cinder-block prison. The ambient sounds of the outdoors were close, which meant she was either in a one-room building, like a storage shed, or an exterior room in a larger building. Either way, she knew if she could get past this wall, she'd be outside.

One step closer to freedom.

But first, she had to get out of this room.

She didn't hear the sound of breathing, as she had in the van. She hoped that meant she was alone, at least for now. She made herself relax, made herself take several deep breaths to calm her raging adrenaline rush. Her heartbeat slowed, not to normal but to something less frantic than the flat-out gallop that had left her feeling shaky and weak. The tremble in her limbs began to subside and her mind began to clear, as well.

Whatever else she knew about the men who'd taken her captive, one thing was clear. They didn't have Danny. They just wanted him. But why? If they didn't have him, who did?

A furtive scraping noise set her nerves jangling again, and she tried to freeze in place, tried to regain her hard-earned calm. But a soft rush of air flowing over her and the faint sound of footsteps on the dirt floor told her she was no longer alone.

"Who's there?" she asked, turning her head toward the sound on instinct, though she could see nothing but a marginal change in the gloom of her cinder-block prison.

The footsteps drew close, and she heard the soft snick of a knife blade snapping open. A large hand circled her wrists, making her jump.

"Don't move and be quiet."

For a moment, she was certain she'd lost her mind. Then she heard the rasp of a blade on plastic and her hands fell free. A quick tug later, the pillowcase was off her head, and she was staring into the most beautiful pair of melted-chocolate eyes she'd ever seen.

"Let's get the hell out of here," Anson said, tugging her to her feet.

Chapter Seventeen

"Do you know where we are?" In the still woods, Ginny's whisper seemed impossibly loud.

Anson took a quick look around the woods to make sure nobody was around to hear, then he turned to look at her. "That building you were in is part of what's left of the old sawmill on Fowler Rise."

Her eyes narrowed. "They don't know where Danny is."

"Yeah, I had a feeling they didn't. I think they were planning to use you as bait to get Danny to show his hand." He tightened his grip on her hand. "I left my car parked just off the road. I'm hoping your buddies in camo didn't spot it and disable it."

"How did you find me?"

A snap of a twig nearby sent Anson's nerves on edge. He pulled Ginny closer, wrapping himself around her protectively as he looked around the thick woods that surrounded them. He saw nothing, but the hair on the back of his neck prickled to attention.

"What is it?" she whispered, her breath warm against his neck.

"I'm not sure," he admitted, willing himself to keep moving. Even if there was someone in the woods watching them, standing still wasn't exactly a stellar plan for getting away unscathed. They needed to get to his car and get back to the safe house. Let Quinn and his agents handle bringing down the bad guys. Anson was a computer geek and Ginny was an accountant.

Crime fighting was definitely not part of their skill sets.

Ginny scrambled gamely to keep up with Anson's longer strides, he noted with pride. His girl was a gamer.

His girl. The idea hit him hard, making him falter for a couple of steps before he pulled himself together again.

His girl. She was his girl. At least, he hoped like hell she was.

"I can't believe you went up there alone to get me," she said a few minutes later as they started across a narrow stream. Only a few hundred yards from where he'd parked his car, he thought, recognizing the landmark. They were almost there.

"Well, I'd have loved to wait for the cavalry, but they weren't in place yet. And I didn't really intend to rescue you alone—I was just staying there until Quinn and the others could make their move. But then those guys walked off and left you all alone—"

"You saw your opening?"

"One of the first rules of gaming. Always take advantage of your opponent's mistakes."

She grinned at him suddenly, creating sunlight in the gloomy woods surrounding them. "You brilliant, geeky genius."

"Well, we haven't won the game yet," he warned, tugging her hand as he started across the remaining distance between him and the place where he'd hidden his car.

He had been afraid the vehicle wouldn't be where he'd left it, but it was there, and after a quick check of the tires and a peek under the hood, he decided it seemed to be untouched. "Get in," he told Ginny as he rounded to the driver's side.

Safely inside the car, he took a moment to turn on his phone. Almost immediately, it started humming with message alerts. The first two were from Quinn, sternly complaining about his sudden penchant for playing action hero.

The third one, however, hit him like a sucker punch to the gut.

"What is it?" Ginny asked.

He turned to look at her, his heart pounding

with dread. How was he supposed to tell her this news?

Her eyes darkened in response to whatever she saw in his expression. "Anson, you're scaring me."

"The police have found Danny."

She stared at him. "And?"

He shook his head.

For a second she just stared at him. Then tears filled her eyes and she looked as if she'd just been floored by the same gut punch that had left him feeling sick. "No."

"I'm so sorry, Gin."

"Who sent the message? Was it Quinn?"

"Adam Brand. He said Quinn wants us to meet him at your place."

"No." She shook her head firmly. "I need to see Danny."

"I'm sure Quinn's going to arrange that. We just need to get to your place first and see what Quinn knows. Okay?"

Tears began to pour down her face. "This isn't

possible. Why would they kill him now? I thought whoever had him was on Danny's side."

Anson didn't know the answer. Maybe they'd been wrong to assume Danny had aligned himself with whoever had him. Just because he'd seemed to go with his abductor willingly didn't mean he wasn't still an expendable pawn. Obviously, he had been or he'd still be alive.

He reached across to touch Ginny's arm, but she pulled away. "Please," she murmured.

He dropped his hand to the keys in the ignition and started the car.

"WE CAN'T GET through to Daughtry." Nick Darcy turned to look at Quinn as soon as he stepped foot in the large central bull pen his field agents called home when they weren't out on assignments. A dozen other agents were there with Darcy—the new hire, Rigsby, plus Cain Dennison, Adam Brand, Seth Hammond and Mark Fitzpatrick and half his field-agent contingent. Olivia Sharp rose with elegant urgency from the corner of Fitzpatrick's desk and crossed to meet him.

"The GPS tracker was at a slightly different position than the last time I checked. Maybe a hundred yards or so from where it was previously, based on the program's calculations. It hasn't moved in about fifteen minutes."

"What does that mean?" Quinn asked.

"Either the car moved and the tracker somehow dropped from where it was attached, or someone moved it deliberately so we couldn't track the car."

Quinn frowned. "And Daughtry still isn't answering his phone?"

"Goes straight to voice mail."

Damn it. What the hell was going on? Had his IT director gone rogue? Now of all times? "Tell me you were able to warn him about the composite sketch before you lost contact."

"No, unfortunately."

Quinn growled a profanity. "He trusts the guy. He could be walking right into a trap."

"We know that," Darcy said, his dark eyes serious.

"Well, what are we going to do about it?" Quinn barked.

HE COULDN'T BE GONE. Not like this. Not so suddenly, in such a stupid, meaningless way.

Ginny pressed the heels of her hands to her burning eyes, willing away the fiery tears and the trembling weakness that Anson's words had evoked. She had to stay strong. It was the least she owed her brother.

Someone had taken him from her too damn soon, and she was going to figure out a way to find them and make them pay, if it was the last thing she did. And this time, she wasn't going to have to handle her troubles alone. She had Anson, Quinn and everybody at The Gates to help her do it.

She looked at Anson as he pulled the car into the gravel drive in front of her small bungalow. "I'm sorry," she said. Even though she spoke softly, the words seemed to ring in the tense silence that had fallen between them.

Anson cut the engine and turned to look at her. "For what?"

"For pulling away when you tried to comfort me."

"It's okay."

She shook her head. "No, it's not. It's just— I'm used to doing everything by myself. Even when Danny—" Her voice broke, but she forced herself to keep going. "Even when Danny was with me, it was still like being alone. I couldn't depend on him—"

She had to stop again, tears burning acid paths down her cheeks.

"You're not alone." Anson unbuckled his seat belt and leaned toward her, sliding his arm around her shoulders. "You don't have to be alone now."

She unlatched her own seat belt and twisted so that he could pull her closer, ignoring the parking brake lever digging into her ribs as she let him hold her for a long, comforting moment.

Finally, he eased apart from her. "We need to go see what Quinn wants. Get things rolling."

She knew he was right, even though she dreaded the next part of her story. Dealing with the minutiae of death. Of final goodbyes. She'd done it with her mother when she was just twenty-two years old. She hadn't thought she'd have to do it again so soon.

"Did Brand say anything about how Danny died?" she asked as she and Anson climbed the porch stairs.

"No. I'm sorry. I guess you'll hear everything as soon as—"

The sound of the front door opening stopped Anson midsentence. She looked up to find herself looking at Marty Tucker standing in the open doorway.

Holding a pistol aimed straight at Anson's heart.

Tuck smiled at them, his grin feral and terrifying. "Good God, I thought you'd never get here," he said.

QUINN'S PHONE RANG as he walked through Anson Daughtry's loft apartment, looking for any sign that his errant IT director had been there in the past day. "Quinn," he answered, not bothering with the code words since he saw Cain Dennison's name on the phone display.

"We found the GPS tracker. It had been removed and tossed into the woods not far from where we think Daughtry parked his car. We dusted for prints, but it was wiped clean."

Great. Quinn passed his hand over his eyes. "Did someone check the sawmill?"

"There were signs that Ginny had been there. And we spotted a couple of bearded guys driving away like bats outta hell in a pickup. I got the license and called Sara to see if she could run the plates. Haven't heard back from her yet."

"Get on back here. We either need to find Daughtry and Ginny or Tuck as quickly as possible."

And hope like hell they hadn't yet run across each other.

He hung up the phone and looked around him, taking in the shabby sofa, the mismatched furnishings, the general air of bachelor disarray, and felt an unaccustomed sense of fear burning in the center of his chest. He had spent twenty years in the CIA running agents and operations like chess pieces on a board, and he'd learned to live with the doubts and regrets by reminding himself that the agents he placed in the field were all there willingly, with open eyes and no illusions.

But Anson Daughtry and Ginny Coltrane weren't agents. Anson was a computer genius and Ginny was an accountant in his payroll department. Their skills were cursory at best, inadequate for the danger they were in.

What kind of danger had he put them in? And how the hell was he going to get them out of it?

Think, Quinn. Anson and Ginny hadn't come here to his place. They hadn't shown up back at the safe house or The Gates.

Where would they go? Or more to the point,

where might Tucker lure them that would seem like a safe place to go?

Home. The word popped into his mind.

Ginny would go home.

"WHERE'S DANNY?" ANSON ASKED, trying to ignore the panic hammering at the back of his throat. He had to remain calm and focused. Ginny's life depended on it. Tuck wouldn't have lured them here if there wasn't something he wanted from them. He could have killed them at any point of this stupid game.

But he's revealed himself now, a mean little voice in the back of Anson's head reminded him. *That means he doesn't intend to leave any witnesses.*

Didn't change the immediate issue, Anson decided, pushing that voice away for the moment. Tuck still needed them alive for now.

But for what?

"He's safe." Tuck looked pointedly at Ginny. "For now."

"What do you want?" she asked.

"The rest of Danny's stash."

Ginny met Tuck's gaze with surprising calm. "What stash?"

"Anson flushed about a kilo of high-grade coke. But Danny stole at least three kilos from the BRI boys for me. I want the rest of it. He says he told you where to find it."

Ginny's reaction to Tuck's reply was minimal. Just a slight twitch of her eyelashes betrayed her surprise, but it was enough for Anson to feel the echo of her pain in his own chest. "Danny told you that?" she asked.

"You're telling me he was lying?" Tuck took a step closer to her.

"Tuck—" Anson moved forward, trying to put himself between Ginny and Tuck's weapon, but Tuck swung the pistol toward him, a dark, warning look in his gray eyes.

"You're not hero material, Anson. You know that as well as I do. So don't try it."

"It's okay, Anson." Ginny put her hand on his

arm, keeping him from moving forward any farther. "I know where to look for the drugs."

Tuck's eyes narrowed as he focused on Ginny again. "You're not jerking my chain, are you? Because that would be a bad idea."

"I'm not," she said calmly, never dropping her gaze from Tuck's. "I know where the drugs are hidden. I was hoping they'd stay hidden for good and nobody would ever find them, but if that's the price for Danny's life—"

"It is," Tuck said flatly.

"Then I guess I'll live with the consequences." She glared at him a moment, then looked at Anson. "Anson isn't part of this, Tuck. He's done nothing wrong. Let him go."

"You know I can't do that."

"Quinn will figure out that it's you."

"He already has," Tuck said. "That's why I need to get this done quickly. And get out of here while I can."

"Stop now and there are no real charges against you," Anson said, trying to appeal to the Marty

Tucker he'd considered his friend. "Nobody saw you coldcock Dale Murdock. No proof you were even there. And the only thing Quinn knows for sure is that you got Danny out of the hospital."

"He won't stop until he can prove everything else. You know what I did to the computer system. That alone is enough to press charges."'

"Turn yourself in. Tell the cops who you were working with and testify against them. Make a deal."

Tuck laughed bleakly. "I'd get jail time either way. I can't be in jail. I'd never make it in there. A guy like me?"

"Why Ginny?" Anson asked. "Why did you implicate her?"

"Because I knew about her taking work home. I realized it was a way to plant that rootkit and get access to all the parts of The Gates' system that nobody but you and Quinn could access."

"You set me up to be a suspect in the mole investigation,"

"That was unfortunate," Tuck said, sounding

almost sincere. "I had to get control of the system to find out everything I needed to know about Quinn's investigation of my friends. The only way to do that was to get you out of the top job. And thanks to Ginny's conscientiousness and Danny's addiction, I was able to do it without implicating myself." He shot them a wry grin. "I'd have gotten away with it if it weren't for you meddling kids—"

"Let's just get this over with," Ginny interrupted. "I'll take you to the drugs. Then you can tie us up and make your getaway. Sell the drugs and head for Mexico or Canada or wherever you're planning to go."

"Good idea," Tuck said with another feral smile that left Anson in no doubt that he didn't intend either of them to get out of this thing alive.

He could see in Ginny's sober blue eyes that she knew it, as well.

But she still lifted her head and nodded toward the back of the house. "This way," she said and started walking down the hall toward the back door.

Tuck nudged Anson ahead of him with the barrel of the gun and followed.

FEARING A STANDOFF, Quinn and four of his armed agents headed on foot down the narrow two-lane road that led to Ginny Coltrane's small house in Two Souls Hollow. As they got a visual on the house, Quinn spoke quietly into his shoulder-mounted radio. "Daughtry's car is parked in front. Nobody inside."

Four short bursts of static came from the other agents. Message received. Only Quinn was to speak through the radios unless someone else got a visual on their targets. All five men were using earbuds to minimize the noise, but voices carried in the woods.

Quinn approached the house at an angle, trying to avoid the direct line of sight out of the windows at the front and side of the house, in case Marty Tucker was watching. As he reached the edge of the porch, he listened carefully for any sounds coming from within the house.

He heard nothing.

"Advance," he murmured quietly into the radio.

The other four men, clad in woodland camo, glided out of the woods like wraiths, taking position at each corner of the house. Adam Brand joined Quinn at his position, making eye contact. At the other corner of the porch, Mark Fitzpatrick raised his head above porch level and made eye contact, as well. Quinn nodded to him and thumbed on the shoulder radio.

"On three," Quinn said. "One. Two. Three."

Brand, Fitzpatrick and Quinn each vaulted onto the porch, trying to make minimal noise beyond the inevitable creak of the wood slats beneath their weight. Brand checked through the window while Quinn eased over to the front door and tried the door handle. It moved effortlessly in his hand.

Bringing his weapon to bear, he pushed open the door and went in fast and low. He heard the back door bang open somewhere on the opposite end of the house. Behind him, Brand and Mark Fitzpatrick entered and spread out, covering the front room.

Room by room, Quinn and his agents carefully checked the house for occupation. But nobody was there.

"Clear," Quinn said finally as they gathered in the hallway.

"I saw footprints in the back," Dennison said. "Looked like at least two sets, maybe three. Heading into the woods. Not sure how long they've been there, though."

"Well, let's take a look, shall we?" Quinn started briskly toward the back of the house, leaving his agents to fall in line behind him.

"YOU AREN'T TAKING me on some kind of snipe hunt, are you?" Tuck's quiet voice inquired, the taunting tone sending a shiver down Ginny's spine.

"We're almost there," she replied as she hiked

up the rise at a steady pace, wishing she felt a little more confident in the plan she'd concocted on the spur of the moment back there in the front room of her house. When Tuck had told her Danny said she knew where to find the drugs, she'd come close to falling apart then and there. And if Anson hadn't been there, needing her to hold it together, she probably would have.

How could Danny have put her in that position? He knew damn well she didn't know anything about his drugs. She didn't even know if there really were two more kilos of cocaine hidden somewhere in or around her house. It might have been a lie Danny told Tuck to take the heat off himself.

That was who her brother had become. It was what the alcohol and maybe even drugs had done to him.

He wasn't the sweet brother she'd known. Not anymore.

She was in this thing by herself.

Except she wasn't, was she? Anson was with

her. Sweet, smart, heroic Anson, who'd saved her twice so far.

Now it was her turn to save him.

"There." She pulled to a halt and pointed ahead, where trees and underbrush fell away to reveal a dark opening in the hillside.

"A cave?" Tuck asked, sounding skeptical.

"Not just any cave," she answered, heading for the cave opening. "Two Souls Cavern."

"Is that supposed to mean something to me?" Tuck asked as he pushed Anson ahead of him and joined her at the mouth of the cave.

She looked over her shoulder at him, taking in the barrel of his gun pointed directly at the back of Anson's neck. She tried not to shudder as she turned back to the dark opening in front of her. "Two Souls Hollow was named that because of the ghosts of Annie Jeffries and Philip Donovan. Young lovers who died in this very cave, hiding from their feuding families."

"Died how?" Tuck asked.

"Suicide pact." Ginny started walking into the cave. "Don't suppose you brought a flashlight?"

"You should have told me we'd need it," Tuck said.

"I think I can find it anyway." She took a step forward and pretended to stumble, crying out loudly.

Two things happened in quick succession. Anson dashed forward to catch her before she fell, his hands closing around her arms.

And a loud rushing noise began to echo through the cave as a writhing black mass moved rapidly toward them.

"What the—" Tuck gasped.

Ginny grabbed Anson's hand. "Run," she growled and pulled him along with her toward the cave opening as the rushing sound crystallized into the roar of hundreds of flapping wings, and the black mass began to break apart, small, leathery-winged bats dipping toward the intruders.

"Son of a bitch!" Tuck cried and began firing his gun at the bats.

The whistling sound of the bullets ricocheting against the stone walls of the cave spurred Ginny to run harder. Anson pulled level with her and they raced through the woods toward the house.

Another gunshot sounded behind them, and Tuck cried out in pain.

"Just keep running," Anson called, tugging harder on her hand.

Suddenly, the woods ahead erupted into movement as five camouflage-clad figures emerged to surround them. Ginny slid to a halt and stared into a familiar pair of hazel-green eyes staring out from a camouflage-streaked face.

"Where's Tucker?" Quinn asked.

"In a cave about a hundred yards back," Anson answered for her.

"He might be injured but he's definitely armed."

Quinn nodded for the other four agents to head in that direction, while he took Ginny's arm and pulled her with him back toward the house. Anson held on to her hand as he kept pace.

"Anything on Danny?" she asked once they were inside the house.

Quinn turned to look at her. "He turned himself in to the Ridge County Sheriff's Department just under an hour ago. They've booked him and taken him back to the hospital for observation."

A flood of relief swamped her, making her knees tremble. "And he's going to be okay?"

"Physically, yes." Quinn met her gaze, his expression uncharacteristically gentle. "But he's got legal issues to deal with. Which will be easy compared to his addiction problem."

Anson stepped closer to her, the heat of his body warm against her back. He closed his large hands over her shoulders, steadying her. "One step at a time," he murmured in her ear.

Not caring that Quinn was there to see it, she turned around and threw her arms around Anson, burying her face in his chest. He wrapped his arms around her so tightly it felt as if he never intended to let her go.

Good, she thought, rubbing her face against the solid warmth of his chest and listening to the beat of his heart in her ear.

Because she never intended to let him go, either.

Epilogue

"I'm sorry. I'm so, so sorry."

Cleaned up and nearly two weeks sober, Danny Coltrane looked and sounded like a different man, but Anson knew how easily an addict could go back to his addictions. Getting clean wasn't nearly as difficult as staying clean.

But for Ginny's sake, he hoped like hell that Danny would be one of the ones who made it.

"I know. I hope you remember how this feels the next time you're tempted to drink or snort or—"

"I will. I promise, I will."

Ginny looked up at Anson. He smiled at her, hoping he looked more confident of Danny's earnestness than he felt. In her eyes, he saw that he hadn't been entirely successful. But she smiled at him anyway, to show she didn't hold his doubt against him.

"The DA is going to recommend a drug treatment facility in Nashville." Danny ran his fingers lightly over the nicked interview table in the Ridge County Sheriff's Department. Sara Dennison—fresh off a four-day honeymoon with her new husband—had listened to Anson's plea and arranged for the meeting to take place away from the county jail visitation room. He knew how disturbing Ginny found seeing Danny through bullet-resistant glass reinforced by wire mesh and talking to him over the phone.

It was Sara who entered a moment later and shot Ginny an apologetic look. "Time's up."

Danny reached across the table and took his sister's hands. "I'm going to make you proud of me again."

She smiled and nodded. "You do that."

Anson rose with her and they remained in the

interview room, side by side, as Sara escorted Danny out. As the door closed behind them, Ginny turned and pressed her forehead against Anson's shoulder.

"I know it's a long shot," she murmured.

"It might happen." He dropped a kiss against her hair.

She leaned her head back and gazed up at him, her eyes the soft blue of a morning sky. "I don't know if I could get through this without you."

"Sure you could." He pushed her hair back from her face. "But you don't have to."

"Good." She smiled the first genuine smile he'd seen from her all day. It warmed him to the bone.

"Quinn texted me before we came in here," he said as he walked her out of the room and into the hallway, sliding his arm over her shoulder and keeping her close. "Tuck's been released from the hospital into police custody."

One of Tuck's wild shots in the cave had ricocheted to hit him in the leg. It had been touch and go for a few days, as the bullet had nicked an artery and only the fast triage work of the four agents who'd found him had kept him alive long enough for paramedics to arrive and get him to the trauma center in Knoxville. But he was going to keep the leg—and what was left of the life he'd ruined with his greed.

"Do you think he'll give up his colleagues?" she asked as he opened the front door for her and led her out into the warm spring sunshine.

"Probably not. I think he sees it as some sort of badge of honor. Not being a snitch." Anson shrugged and followed her to where he'd parked his car. He opened her door for her and walked around to the driver's side.

Ginny remained outside the car, gazing at him over the top of the vehicle, her eyes narrowed against the midday brightness.

"What?" he asked when she didn't speak right away.

"I think I'm in love with you," she said soberly.

The words caught him by surprise. Not the emotion so much—she'd been showing him just how much she cared for him for the past two weeks, in small ways and spectacular ones. But he'd begun to doubt she'd ever say the words aloud, knowing how wary she was of making herself so vulnerable to another person, especially after her brother's betrayal.

He felt a slow smile spread over his face as she gazed back at him, waiting for him to respond. "I know," he said.

She frowned. "You just went Han Solo on me. You insufferable geek."

His grin broadened. "Get in the car, Leia."

She slid into the passenger seat as he took his place behind the steering wheel. They buckled up in silence, but before he put the keys in the ignition, he turned to look at her, waiting until she turned to meet his gaze.

"You know that feeling you get when you finish reconciling your balance sheet and everything matches the very first time?" he asked.

A smile flirted with her lips. "Love that feeling," she admitted.

He nodded. "When I look at you, when I even think of you, that's how I feel. Times a thousand."

Her smile spread until it nearly blinded him. "You are such a romantic, Anson Daughtry."

Grinning, he started the car. "I am," he agreed. "I really am."

* * * * *